AND THE STARS WEPT

Chloe Helton

PULSE

Published by Propel,
an imprint of Pulse

www.pulsepub.net
info@pulsepub.net

And the Stars Wept is a work of fiction. Names, characters, places, and incidents either are the product of the author's imagination or are used fictitiously. Any resemblance to actual persons living or dead, events, or locales is entirely coincidental. All opinions expressed in this work are purely for fictional purposes and do not represent the opinions of the author or the publisher.

Published and printed in
United States Of America

To my father, who taught me to love the sweat and blood,
and to my mother, whose caring hand was an invaluable guide.

Chapter One

Illinois, 1861

The day Joshua ran away was the day of my father's last breath.

Kneeling beside his creaky bed, I was pressing a damp cloth to my father's head when I became aware of my brother's conspicuous absence. The whole house seemed empty without Joshua's presence as if it had begun to sag. When his footsteps did not boom around the small cluster of rooms and when his newly deep voice did not echo across the walls, it was difficult not to notice.

Of course, I could not tell Father he was gone. I could not leave to find him, either. Such was my dilemma, and fervent prayers whenever my father momentarily closed his eyes did nothing to help the problem.

"Where's your brother?" Father croaked once, as the sun began to set. "I have something to tell him."

"I think he's away at the moment, Father." That, at least, was not a lie. "Gathering firewood. He'll be back soon." *That* was a lie.

Joshua had run away. I knew it because he never left the house without telling me, and he had been especially jittery in the last few days as it became unavoidably clear that our father was not going to get better. Since the war first broke out, Joshua had spoken of the soldiers as if they were heroes. When we saw the first ones off on that fateful Sunday, he must have cheered the loudest in the whole town—I could hardly hear afterward. After that, he would mention them occasionally. Whenever he was angry, whenever he had to do work he didn't want to, he would mutter something that usually sounded like, "I wish I were a goddamned soldier," though I could never be quite sure of the exact words.

So, yes, I knew he had run away, and I was quite afraid of what that meant. But for as long as I could hear Father's labored breathing and feel his faint heartbeat through his chest, I would be here.

"Good of him," Father mumbled, and it was a moment before I remembered our conversation. "It's getting colder. You'll need to be warm tonight."

"You, especially, will need to be warm," I added, confused at his wording.

Father shook his head as if I didn't understand but said nothing.

I focused on how I would later explain our lack of firewood and how I would distract him from Joshua's absence. The last thing he needed right now was to wonder if his son was wandering lost in the woods. Could I tell him that Joshua had gone to town? We did need more food; he would probably believe it. The lie, even if unspoken, already felt thick in my chest, but it would be much better than telling him the truth.

"You're quite a handsome young woman," my father said in broken breaths that took me a moment to understand. "You look just like your mother."

I turned away.

"I appreciate that," I replied as I shook out the rag.

"I never told you that before, but you look just like her."

These were words I didn't want to hear. Was he going to spill his whole heart to me now? Was he going to tell me about all the things he wished he had done better, all the praise he had left unspoken, all the beatings he could have saved us? I hoped he kept it quiet; I didn't want to hear his regrets or his apologies. I just wanted to mourn him without having to think about these things.

Day drooped into night. Minute by minute, hour by hour, I was losing him.

When it had finally become dark enough for me to light the lantern, Father croaked again, "Where is Joshua?"

"He should be back any minute," I lied.

His snort, though quiet, radiated disbelief. "You don't have to lie to me anymore, Cassandra."

"I'm not—"

"It doesn't matter. Tell him something for me, okay? Tell him I'm proud that he has finally become a man."

Finally, he had said. Was that an insult, or at least a backhanded sort of compliment?

"When he comes back, you can tell him that."

"Ah, Cassandra, we both know that he won't be back in time."

"I'm sorry," I said, bowing my head. I wanted to cry. "I'm sorry."

"You probably don't understand why he did it," Father said, "but luckily, I do. The little bastard."

"Why is it, then?"

"It doesn't matter. As long as you tell him what I've told you, I will be fine."

I nodded, still upset. Even if Father was not angry with him, it was still a heartless thing for Joshua to do. And what could possibly be the reason to run away on his dying father? What could be more important than saying good-bye?

"Cassandra," Father croaked, hours later, "I'm proud of you, too."

I had been kneeling by the bedside, the lantern at my ankles, staring into its light while muttering a fervent prayer in order to keep myself awake. Now, I shot up and hovered over my father.

"No," I said, panicking. "No, not now." I reached for his hand. "Not yet!"

He squeezed it gently. Comfortingly.

"Father, stay with me," I pleaded. "It is not your time."

He shook his head and smiled peacefully, not speaking a single word. This could not be, it could not be, it could not be.

Yet, it was. His eyelids drifted shut, his skin turned cold, and his pulse disappeared. Neither Joshua, nor Father, even, had apparently considered this: I was alone now, in the dead of night, with only the body of my father for company. It was an aching, painful loneliness. And every time the wind whispered through the trees, every time the house creaked, I was convinced that God was coming for me, too.

Joshua was a predictable creature, so it wasn't hard to guess where he had gone. The next morning, I dragged my father's body outside and placed him in a shallow grave—one that could be dug up easily if we were to come back and hold a funeral with a few neighbors, but also one that would keep if we didn't—and then I set off for the town.

Our town was small enough, so I could expect many questions if I came across someone we knew: *what brings you to town today? how is your dear father doing? is he well?* How would I answer these?

The post office was fairly busy—half a dozen people crowded about, chatting conspiratorially. It was not Sunday, so it wasn't as if the whole town had turned up to gossip, but it wasn't unusual for people to stop and chat a bit whenever they came, especially because few of us did it very often.

"I heard they're sending another group out in a few weeks," Mrs. Perry, one of our closer neighbors, reported. "Have you seen the dailies? Lincoln is calling for more men. Seems this war won't end as quickly as we thought."

Her companion, the widow Miss Eliza, sniffed.

"It's an awful thing. If only those Carolinian traitors had held their tongues—"

They both turned to me as I drew closer.

"Oh, hello, Cassandra." Mrs. Perry smiled. "What brings you

to town today?"

I cleared my throat. What could I possibly tell her? "Oh, nothing of note," I said. "Just the usual." Whatever that meant.

"Where is your father? Surely he has come with you."

I shook my head. "Father is at home. He's rather ill. Joshua and I came up to visit the butcher, but I seem to have lost him. Have you seen him?"

Miss Eliza blinked. "Oh."

Mrs. Perry turned to her. "What is it, Eliza?" "Oh, dear. Your brother can't be the one who was here yesterday, can he?"

"I fail to understand what you mean," I replied, my heart speeding up.

"Well, I was here at the post office yesterday, and I saw someone—he looked like he was talking about enlistment. I could have sworn he looked like your Joshua, but then I thought, *"No, it cannot be."* Surely, it was not actually him?"

"He's not of age," I replied, though this was probably not the answer she was looking for. "He cannot enlist."

"I do hope I have not distressed you, Cassandra, because it cannot possibly have been him."

I shook my head. "No," I agreed, "it cannot have been."

I bid the now-suspicious women a quick, shaky farewell and dashed into the post office. It was a little building, hardly bigger than the shed in our backyard, with a single window and only enough room for one desk and the scruffy-haired clerk who occupied it. I had a few memories of this place, mostly of receiving letters from distant family, but Father hardly ever brought me into town when he came and besides, we never got letters often anyhow. However, it was enough that I was vaguely familiar with this clerk; he probably recognized my face even if he did not know my name.

"What do you want?" the man asked, not rudely, but hardly kindly, either.

"I'm trying to find my brother, and I think he might have tried to enlist in the army. His name is Joshua Clark."

He regarded me gruffly. "Well, what do you want me to do about it?"

"Have you seen him? He would have come in yesterday, late afternoon. He's a tall, skinny, brown-haired boy. Looks about sixteen."

"I don't remember him."

"Well, is it possible that he still did come in? Can I take a look at the enlistment log? There must be one."

He sighed and reached for a thick book at the corner of the desk, lazily pushing it toward me. "Have a look if you want."

I flipped through the pages. There had to be at least a dozen names—that was a quarter of the town's men already. Had they all been sent out already? Some of these names must have been from several months ago when everyone panicked after the firing on Fort Sumter. We hadn't sent out many men, but I was sure we'd sent some. And what had happened to them?

On the last page, I scrolled through the scrawled, hardly legible names: *Henry, Johnny, Caleb…* I didn't see a Joshua.

"Maybe he wrote down a different name," I suggested.

"Well, miss, I wouldn't know."

"When is the next group being sent out?"

"At the end of the month. That's when they'll get their uniforms and their rations."

I didn't even know what a ration was.

"Are you sure you didn't see him? Can you remember anything about the people who came in yesterday?"

"If I did," he replied roughly, "I would have said so, wouldn't I?"

I closed the book and slid it back to him. "I'm sorry, sir. I hope I haven't been a bother."

He shook his head as I exited through the door.

Well, perhaps Joshua *hadn't* enlisted. That was a relief. But where was he, then? Had he gone to the next town to enlist because nobody would recognize him there? I wondered if that was even possible. Perhaps the next town over would not allow him to enlist if they had never seen him before. They would know he didn't live there. But did it matter?

I stopped in my tracks and glanced about me. I was in the middle of the town, still in sight of the post office, and I peered across at the short row of buildings that made our little village. A bakery, a butcher's shop, a general store, and a few trade shops. And, of course, the pub. If Joshua was here, it wouldn't be hard to find him. And he had to be here—where else would he go? I highly doubted that he had actually made the trek to the next town. He wouldn't have left me here.

Thus I wandered about, asking after my brother and finding nothing. I did not even think to look in the pub—though the thought did spin at the back of my mind. It was midday, after all. There was no reason for anyone to be there, much less my under-aged brother. The thought of Joshua in a place like that made my stomach ill.

Well, I had looked everywhere else. It was worth a try.

The place was dark and musty, and the predictable stench of alcohol assaulted my nose. I was certainly familiar with the smell—Pa had never shied from the bottle—but it was uncomfortable all the same.

"Can I help you?" the bartender asked.

"Yes, I'm looking for my brother. Have you possibly seen him?" I gave my standard description: tall, thin, brown-haired.

The bartender seemed annoyed, probably because I wasn't buying anything.

"Yeah," he sighed. "I think I know whom you're talking about. He's out back."

I wondered if Joshua had actually purchased any alcohol. It

seemed like just the sort of naive thing he would do, and this bartender seemed like a man who would glance aside at the fact that Joshua was clearly too young. Ignoring my impulse to further interrogate this man, I bid him thanks and sought my brother.

And there he was, standing casually behind the building, arms crossed, staring at the sky.

I grabbed Joshua by the collar and slammed him against the pub wall.

"You," I panted, "are being incredibly stupid."

The grief, the frustration, the confusion—they had overtaken me. Perhaps I was acting a bit harshly. Did I care? No.

"Do you have any idea what you've done?"

He struggled against my loosened grip.

"Cassie! Let me go!"

I let him free but kept my hand on the wall next to him.

"Answer this, Joshua. Did you enlist in the army?"

A bird squawked. Someone in the distance laughed uproariously. My brother nodded slowly.

Using the hand that had settled on the wall, I pounded my fist against the structure.

"How dare you," I hissed. "How dare you run out on Pa. How dare you leave me to deal with him alone. And *how dare you* put yourself in such senseless danger!"

Joshua squirmed beneath my outstretched arm and broke free.

"I had no choice!"

I shook my head incredulously, and he huffed.

"You don't understand."

"You're right, I truly don't."

I rubbed my forehead with two fingers. There were so many things I wanted to say—so many questions, so many complaints, so many demands—that it was hard to decide what to say next.

"Why did they even let you enlist? You're clearly not old enough."

Joshua lifted his chin proudly.

"Obviously, I don't look too young."

How naïve he was.

"We're going back there and crossing off your name."

"No!"

He tried to lurch away, but I grabbed him by the shirt. Joshua struggled valiantly, and I realized how strong he had become. Not so long ago I could wrestle him to the floor without sweating; now I could barely keep my grip on his arm.

"Just give it up!" I started to yell as I struggled to hold him. "You're too young! You don't know what you're doing!"

He shoved himself free.

"Look, Cassie," he said as he panted. "Stop yelling for a minute and listen to me."

"I can't believe you did something so *stupid*—"

"I didn't have a choice!" he yelled. "What else are we going to do? How are we going to feed ourselves?"

"I don't know. We'll figure something out."

"Like what? We both know you won't find anything here."

Our townsfolk were nice, but they hardly had the money to feed themselves, much less hire more workers. Father had supported us before with his farm, just scraping by, and though we had worked for him many years, we didn't have the manpower between the two of us to run it ourselves. I could try—I was seventeen, after all. Or I could get married, and Joshua could live with us until he was old enough to find work for himself. But what were my chances of finding a husband before Joshua and I both starved to death?

"Should we run off to Springfield so we can work ourselves to the bone in a factory?"

I was certain that Joshua didn't know much about working in a factory, and neither did I, but we'd both heard many things about it, and they were not good.

"No, we won't do that."

"Then what? The army is offering thirteen dollars a month, Cassie. We won't have to worry about food anymore!"

"And then what?" I demanded. "You would risk your life for that?"

"Yes," he replied. "Because it's the only way we'll get to eat."

I shook my head. I couldn't believe this, I couldn't *believe* it, but he was right. What else could we do? There was no other certain way to support both of us.

"How are we to stay together? I suppose I could just accompany the army. They must need some kind of help—nurses, cooks, or something."

I slid down the wall until I was sitting, dress billowed out, in a bed of dust. Joshua sat, too, with crossed legs.

"I can't believe this is happening." I laughed darkly. "Two weeks ago we were living happily as ever. We were working with Pa on the farm, and I was wondering if I would be married soon, and now this."

Joshua gulped. "I'm sorry. About everything."

I let my head drop into my hands, cradling it there for a moment, before sitting back up.

"It will be all right," I told him. "There must be another way."

My brother pursed his lips. He was clearly thinking, *"There is no other way."*

"Father told me to tell you this: *I am proud that you have finally become a man.*"

Joshua rubbed his own knee with his thumb.

"Was it peaceful? Was he all right?"

"It was peaceful," I replied, "for him, just like falling asleep."

We sat there for many minutes after. The war, Joshua's enlistment, the problem of our survival—those things hovered over us like spindly branches—like poisonous fruits—waiting to drop. We sat there for many minutes, and we prayed.

Chapter Two

The air was thick with anticipation and the smell of sweat. Every man, woman, and child from here in Greenville or any of the half-dozen nearby hamlets stood as parts of the crowd in the city square: the new soldiers in the center and the women and children all around. Men who were too old or crippled to work were scattered among the women and children, but some of the men going out as soldiers looked like hazards. I spotted a few with missing arms, even missing legs.

"As long as we've got two front teeth," Joshua had told me, "we're allowed to go."

It was for biting the paper off the cartridges. And for God's sake, if I knew that a missing tooth was all it took, I would've broken one of Joshua's myself. Then he'd never be able to go.

I scanned the rows and rows of men in search of him. There were hundreds and hundreds of men, maybe even a thousand. How many would come home? Joshua would. If God had any mercy, any mercy at all, He would bring him home.

At the topmost step of the city hall building, a pastor began to address the men. The crowd grew silent, but I was still too far away to hear him. His face was earnest, and the soldiers seemed moved by it. Try as I did, I could not see my brother among the men.

A small figure brushed the back of my leg. I looked down to see a young boy. He was five or six at most and tall enough to touch my navel. It seemed that he had touched me by accident, but when I looked at him, he began to study me carefully, and I could not tear my eyes from him.

His mother extended a hand to his shoulder and pulled him back.

"My apologies, ma'am," she said as she blushed and cast a stern look toward the child.

"Is your Pa there?" the boy asked, pointing toward the soldiers.

The mother blushed again, and I chuckled sadly.

"No, but my brother is."

"My Pa is there. He's fighting because God told him to."

"God told my brother the same thing." I smiled, wishing it were true. If God had ordered it, I might have some peace.

When my back was turned, I heard the boy whisper to his mother, "Ma, when I'm big, can I be a soldier like Pa?"

"I hope it must never be so," his mother replied quietly.

"But why would God order Pa to be a soldier and not me?"

"Someday, dear, you'll understand."

"I want a rifle like Pa," the boy whispered. "When I'm big, can I have a rifle?"

I could not help but glance back at the mother. With numbness in her eyes, she smiled politely at me, and I turned my head back from embarrassment as she whispered, "Listen to the priest, Henry. He is saying a prayer."

"But can I have a rifle?"

"Shh. Just listen."

As the barely-audible prayer drifted over the thick crowd, I found myself praying, too.

"Lord, give my brother the courage to meet every battle and give me the strength to patch his wounds if need shall be." And so it went on until the sound began to rumble through the crowd once more, and I thought, *"But most of all, Great Father in Heaven, bring my brother home."*

It took me a moment to realize, but the men were singing: "Sweet land of liberty, of thee I sing." And just as Henry's voice sounded in my ear, not quite in tune and not with all the right words but earnest nevertheless, I lent mine to the song, too.

"Land where my fathers died, land of the Pilgrims' pride, from every mountainside let freedom ring."

Soon every voice carried the song, and it must have echoed for miles and miles. I didn't know the rest of the words, but I sang as best I could, and by the time we started to hurrah, there were tears in my eyes, silent sobs seizing my body between shouts. I was weeping.

"Three cheers for the Union! Hip-hip-hurrah! Hip-hip-hurrah! Hip-hip-hurrah!"

Pots and pans clanked, and men laughed gaily in the great commotion of supper. They piled a measly bit of meat and a block of hardtack onto their empty dishes. The rations were slightly less than decent, not little enough to complain but not up to the standard of what one would consider satisfactory. You would have thought, however, that the men were eating like kings. I caught bits of the conversation.

"You gonna take your time with that, eh, Timothy?"

"It's looking good tonight. You ever had hardtack, Tom? Neither have I."

"I'm gonna try to write to her as soon as we finish. I know, it's only been a day! She misses me already, trust my word."

Joshua was third in line now. I watched as he moved up the front, and I knew exactly what he was thinking as he collected the rations: *"Oh, that does look good. But is it too much? I probably can't have three pieces. I've only seen anybody take one so far. Maybe I can get away with two?"*

It was always a fine line with the two of us. Take as much as you can without appearing impolite. Not that we ever had occasion to use such manners, except for visits to Mona. We'd been there four times, perhaps five. Once, Joshua had taken two whole legs of chicken for himself—it was the time of life when boys grow at immeasurable rates and they never stop being hungry—and I had slapped him on the hand for it. "Manners," I had said, the way Ma had always done to me. She didn't notice how I scolded him then, but she would have appreciated it. Mona had seen it, though, and had looked away.

"Are you starting to drool, too?" The voice was from beside me, but I only turned my head a bit to look.

"What? Oh, the food. Well, yes, I suppose. We did eat well, though."

"Oh, I'm not saying differently." She laughed. "But I think that no matter how much we have, we'll always be hungry."

It sounded as if I was supposed to understand some deeper meaning.

The sky began to ease into sunset. I hadn't stopped looking at Joshua.

"Do you have a sweetheart out there?" she asked.

"No. I have a brother. Do you?"

"His name's Nicholas. He's by the fire, just sitting down right now. Do you see him? The brown hair."

I nodded, but I had the sense that it didn't really matter to her whether I actually answered.

"He was going to marry me. I'm determined that he still will."

I nodded. "He seems like a fine man."

"If only we could dine with them. I'm sure he's looking for me, too. See, he's looking our way. Nicholas!"

He caught her eye and smiled as she waved. She turned to me, and I felt compelled to do the same.

We were by a campfire, looking on at the camp not so far away. There were a dozen other female nurses and almost as many men, but many of them had gone to bed or had otherwise disappeared. I had expected to see Joshua quite a bit more; it wasn't deeply surprising that they had separated us women from the soldiers, but I had prayed so dearly that we would have a chance to see each other still.

"What do you say we go over there anyway?"

"Are you crazy? What if the captain comes out of his tent?"

"He's got two bottles of liquor and an armful of maps. We won't see him until morning. Trust me," she said as she laughed, "I've been with this company since the war started, and he's never once come back out once he's in for the night."

"What if there's a ruckus?"

"We'll scurry back. Besides, like I said, he won't come out himself. And his lieutenants are pussycats. Come, the men will love us. I'll have my Nicholas, and you'll have your brother, and the rest will be too busy with their cards to care much about us."

"I would rather we just follow orders."

"Orders," she whispered conspiratorially. "Rules are for the men, not for us. Come on!"

I wasn't sure that her philosophy would hold up, but I was dearly tempted to see my brother.

"If we get caught," I hissed as she began to stride toward the men, "I will make you take all of the blame."

"Don't be silly, Anna! We won't be caught."

She was already several paces in front of me. I didn't know where she got the impression that my name was Anna, but frankly, I didn't really care what she called me.

She was sitting beside her Nicholas in seconds. There weren't an awful lot of men in the company, and very few of them looked delighted that Nicholas had a female companion, while the rest of them did not, but the mood changed little. Besides, I was quite convinced that female company was available to them already, albeit of a very different kind.

"Cassie?"

Joshua was playing cards with a group of men who were suspiciously eyeing my uniform. Clearly, they knew I was not supposed to be here.

"I didn't know they allowed nurses in camp."

A companion of his cut in. "They don't. But don't worry, Miss

Cassie, we won't tell."

Joshua put down an ace, and the men roared. Apparently, he had won.

"That's twenty cents for me!" he exclaimed, grabbing coins from atop the tree stump on which they had played.

It seemed unusual that he was already winning money from a simple practice game, but the men seemed happy to indulge him. I wondered if they knew he wasn't of age; I didn't see how anyone could mistake him for eighteen. Seventeen, maybe, but not eighteen. In truth, he was only sixteen.

I hovered awkwardly over the men, not sure whether I was welcome to sit. It was silly of me to expect that Joshua would abandon his game in order to chat with me, but I honestly did expect a bit more attention after I'd broken such a rule to get here. Yet what could I do? He seemed happy; he was fitting in, and I didn't want to take that from him, although that wasn't what we'd come here for.

One of the men scooted sideways to make space and said, "Well, come on, Miss Cassie, sit down with us."

I smiled shyly and maneuvered my skirt over the log.

"My name is Henry," he said.

He was twenty, maybe twenty-one, as far as I could tell, with flaxen hair and a fair face.

"Have you ever played Faro?"

I snorted. I'd only once seen a deck of cards in my life.

"Don't worry, it's very simple."

He proceeded to explain the rules; it seemed that we were, quite plainly, betting on whether a certain card would be placed first or second. There wasn't much skill to it until the end when many cards were already used, and only a few cards were left. I joined the game and started putting coins down. By nightfall, I was empty-handed, and Joshua came away with a near-pocketful of coins.

"Your brother there is a mighty good gambler," Henry commented.

"It must be beginner's luck. I haven't the faintest clue where he would have learned how to gamble."

"Maybe at school. That's where I learned, at least."

I'd never thought of that. I'd stopped going to school when Ma died, so I didn't have much of an education compared to Joshua. I didn't have much of an idea what boys got up to during their lunchtime. The girls had all made flower crowns and staged mock weddings, sometimes claiming a stray boy or two for a groom, but most of the boys had disappeared into the trees until it was time to return. We'd all just assumed they were catching frogs in the creek. I'd never heard a word about gambling.

The men began to disperse to their tents, backpacks in hand, with jolly adieus and mocking comments—all in jest. The other nurse—I really did have to learn her name—was already in the tent when I ducked through the angular flaps.

"How did it go?" she greeted me ever so quietly, her tone unreadable, as not to wake the others.

I sighed. "It went."

She nodded as if she understood completely. Her time with Nicolas seemed to have been quite jolly, and I didn't understand what she could be upset about.

"It's so lonely here," she whispered.

I shrugged in acknowledgment before turning over. I didn't want to talk about it, but she was right.

"Look!" Beth, the other nurse, exclaimed. "Freddie just hit one into the trees."

I glanced at the game. Baseball, it was called. Perhaps it was fun to play (I could imagine myself hitting a ball sky-high, farther than anybody could reach), but it was a drag to watch. Nicholas was the pitcher, though, so Beth couldn't keep her eyes off the game, and she frequently tried to divert my attention from a letter I was writing to Mona despite my polite cues that I was not interested.

"How exciting! I wonder who's up next? Oh, here he comes. Is that your brother?"

I dropped my pen in my lap. A lanky brunette boy took the bat, and despite several yards' distance, it was quite clear that he was indeed Joshua. When the ball came, he used the bat to casually swat it across the field.

"Look at him! Nobody has hit it on the first try so far."

I grinned. "He was always good at games like this."

The next pitch soared through the air. After some quick movement that I couldn't read, Joshua bent over, clutching his hand in apparent misery.

"Joshua!" I cried, surging forward to help him. Beth's arm pulled me back. "What are you doing?" I demanded.

"He's fine, Anna."

God, if she could only learn my real name.

"If he needs help, he'll come to us."

"Will he, though?" I thought. It seemed to me that he would make every effort to stifle any pain. "I have to help him."

"Anna," she repeated. "Let him be."

A quarter of an hour later, after another successful hit by Joshua and a few changes of the bat, the men came trotting from the field. Soon, Nicholas was right beside us and, in a move that I wanted to say was surprising but truly wasn't, Joshua had not come to me. I started to scan the camp, but I felt a creeping uneasiness about Beth. She and Nicholas were chatting casually, but there was something off about her—something I could not explain. She smiled widely, but her eyes were sad; she laughed merrily, but she rubbed her own arms with her hands as if she was trying to shield herself from something. But then she would throw her head back in carefree giggles, and I would wonder if I was really seeing things right.

In front of the crackling campfire, Letitia sipped her coffee and looked around at the circle of us, all rapturously attentive. Letitia was the lead nurse. In our camp hospital, she answered only to the head surgeon, who seemed to have little good feeling for her but respected her all the same. It was hard not to respect her; she was friendly and warm, but she was tougher than a brick wall.

"Tell the Bull Run story!" a nurse named Georgia called.

"I've told it a thousand times," Letitia replied, graciously sipping her coffee again without expression.

"Not everybody's heard it, though. We have so many new ones."

She placed her coffee on her lap.

"Fine, I will tell it. I must warn you that it's not as exciting as Georgia may lead you to think."

She took a deep breath, and we were in a trance.

"I don't know how much you've heard about Bull Run, but it was a horror. All the townspeople and even some nobler men—I swear there was a Congressman there— brought their families and sat down for a nice little picnic to watch the skirmish. Well, they thought it would be a skirmish. I was in the hospital all day, and I can tell you, I served for the war with the Mexicans, and never in all my years there did I see anything as bad as Bull Run. I was used to tents of a few dozen men at most—and let me say, Bull Run was not so much bigger than any of the other battles I'd seen—but now there were hundreds and hundreds of men. Can you even imagine it? Men would come in shouting their throats dry, and I would have to pin them down like dogs so they wouldn't squirm when I gave them the chloroform. The surgeons were no help, either; I was one of only a few women there, and I was as good as a three-legged horse to him, although I probably worked as hard as any male nurse. Oh, all right, Georgia, I'll get there. My purpose here is to show that it was the worst experience of my whole life. There have never been so many wounded men in one place that I can think of. So I was working furiously—from dawn till near dusk with hardly a break to swallow a few crumbs—and I saw so many men come through, but I will tell you the one I remember.

"His name was Bobby Brown. I don't know if that was his real name, God help me, but that's what he told me. He had a bullet through the stomach—we thought there was no way he could make it—and it took so long to dig it out, I was sure that any second I would cut too deep and kill him right there. Thank the Lord that didn't happen. So there I was, carving a bullet out of a dead man, and the whole time he was talking about his father, but it was very odd. 'My Father would never allow this,' he said, 'Don't fret for me, sweet merciful angel, because my Father will not let me die here.' At first, I thought he must be speaking of the Lord, that he was simply being ornate by calling Him '*my* father' instead of '*the* Father.' Oh, and I shouldn't forget the oddest one: 'My Father is my master, and He will avenge those who have harmed me.' Perhaps I was only being fretful, but have you ever heard of anyone speak of the Lord that way? He is not a vengeful creature, and certainly not a 'master,' for we are not His slaves. But I was still not convinced that there was something entirely wrong with him—he was just a little odd, that was all. He was dying, for God's sake—but then I moved him to his side to examine him, and I swear, my heart nearly stopped. You've never seen anything like it in your whole life—his right hand had *six* fingers."

Someone gasped audibly, and my heart did skip a beat.

"And Bobby Brown did live that day. A bullet straight through the stomach—I've never seen another live through something that bad—but he did. He walked out two days later as if he hadn't been injured at all. Can you believe such a thing?"

Beth glanced at me. She had probably heard this story before—she certainly wasn't reeling in surprise as most of us were—but she seemed troubled by it, too. I did not believe that the devil walked among us, but there were certainly sinister things in this world, and it seemed that Bobby Brown was proof of that.

Letitia let her story hang in the air for a few moments before continuing.

"Well, it is late. We have much to do tomorrow, don't we?"

And somehow, within seconds, she was gone.

I gulped and turned to Beth.

"The men will fight tomorrow, yes?"

"If all goes well. Don't worry, you'll be just fine. You won't have to do much except chloroform and bullet wounds because you're new."

I didn't even know what *chloroform and bullets* really meant for me.

"I heard it's the most awful thing in the world, seeing all those wounded men."

"Oh, it is," Beth assured me. "But you'll get used to it. And you'll stop worrying about your brother so much. One gets used to that, too."

The sky was darkening, and the wind howled.

"Don't worry," Beth assured me. "You'll learn quickly. Everything will be all right."

I was not sure if she was lying. Still, as soon as my back touched my sleeping mat, I launched into deep prayer. When the reveille sounded the next morning, I was as anxious as ever.

The man came to me gasping and covered in blood, like a newborn child to its mother.

"Lie there," I told him gently, gesturing to the last empty space.

A saintly old woman had offered the bottom floor of her manor for our use, and there weren't any beds, but the space was so sparsely furnished that we were able to place most of the men across the floor. They kept coming in, though, and there wasn't enough time to drag the dead outside to make room. There was no room to walk even, without stepping over groaning bodies.

I began examining his torso for a wound.

"Where is it?" I asked, my hands roaming across his chest, and he gestured to a spot just below his collarbone.

"God's bones," I breathed, "so close to the heart."

I was pressing gauze into the sprouting blood within seconds. Only this morning, I had been jittery and nervous to see the men, but now I didn't even have time to wipe the sweat off my brow while I bandaged wounds and poured whiskey into weak mouths. I didn't have time to grieve for those who breathed their last in the crimson-stained grass just outside the tent. We could only thank the Lord that it wasn't raining.

"My wife," the man gasped as I continued to stifle the bleeding. "My wife…"

"Sir, don't give up now. There's time yet."

He laughed. "It would take a miracle, darling."

"I've heard of such things," I said, and it wasn't funny, really, but he laughed weakly, and I could feel him weakening. I could feel him slipping away…

No, he couldn't. A few men had died under my watch so far but never right under my hands. I'd never been able to feel the last breath of a person.

"Sir. Sir, stay with me."

It wasn't the calm request of a trained nurse. No, it was the gasping plea of a scared woman. Was I only that, a scared woman? I had to do better.

"My wife," he whispered, "is Mary DeLaurent. Please, if you will, make sure she gets this."

Somehow, despite my figure looming over him, he was able to extract a ring from his finger, and he slipped it into my hand.

"Keep it with you," I told him, "until the very last. All right? I will take it then."

He nodded. "You are a blessed woman."

I grimaced and immediately regretted that I wasn't able to accept the praise properly.

The man began to heave, and I pressed the gauze harder into his chest.

"Shh, shh," I said, "talk to me. What's your name?"

"Bobby. Bobby DeLaurent."

"Okay, Bobby. Tell me about your wife. Tell me about Mary."

He gasped quietly but began to grow calm.

"She's the most beautiful woman to walk this earth. That's nothing on you, darling." He grinned. "But she really is. She's working the farm now—she can do it as well as me, I think, but it's a shame she's got to do everything by herself. I told her I wouldn't be long. Got my six months, you know, and then I'll be home again. But I guess it's not like that now, is it?" He started to breathe heavily again. "I just don't want her to be alone."

"Where does she live, Bobby?"

"Maryland. Close to Washington. I'm in the Maryland 7th." He turned his eyes to the sky. "Just give her the ring. Make sure she knows she won't be alone. She won't be alone. I'll be—" he said as he huffed quietly, "with her."

"I'm going to get you through this, Bobby, okay? You've got to believe me. You've got to believe that you'll be all right."

He laughed. "I may believe in God, darling, but I don't have that much faith. Here, take the ring."

It was now loose in his hand, and he grasped it. I didn't have the heart not to take it.

At that moment Beth rushed in with two more men.

"Bullet to the chest and bullet in the leg."

She was close enough to me to whisper, "The first man's a lost cause, but there may be hope for the second."

I glanced back at Bobby, who nodded his head.

"Go," he said. "Do your duty. I'll be fine."

I had a suspicion, one that sank deep in my chest, that he wasn't telling the truth, but I said, "Pray harder than you've ever prayed, Bobby, and I will pray for you, too."

Then I rushed to Beth's side, slipping the ring into my pocket.

Beth was right about the man with the chest wound, and because she was an angel, she knelt beside him as I tended to the one with the shot leg. I couldn't take another lost cause at the moment. I had to save somebody.

I spotted the new patient's injury right away. Without thinking, I ripped a bit of gauze from the roll in my hand and tied it around the gunshot hole, as tight as I could. At least it wasn't the artery; if it had been, he'd likely be dead by now. As it was, I put all of my weight into my hands as I pressed on the wound. The patient groaned in pain.

"You're going to be all right," I told him quietly but loud enough for Beth to give me a look. Maybe most of the nurses didn't speak to their patients. "You're going to be all right."

He shook his head.

"My—leg," he said, "the bone. I think the bone is shattered."

He was gasping in pain.

I looked at Beth. She really didn't know much more than me, but it was more comforting to have a second opinion.

I turned back to the patient, asking, "Are you sure?" and when he nodded, I asked Beth, "Should I call the surgeon for a shattered bone?"

My friend nodded at the same time as the patient gasped, "Don't let them take it off! Don't let them!"

"Sir, I have to call the surgeon. I'm going to call the surgeon, and he'll decide what to do."

He closed his eyes and nodded.

The hospital steward was, not surprisingly, swamped already and, even though he acknowledged me from across the room when I called his name, I knew that it would be a while before he could come over.

"I have to check on somebody else," I told the patient. "Do you think you can put pressure on the wound for a few minutes?"

He nodded, and I moved his hand to the wound. He was weak, definitely weaker than me, but it would have to do.

I stepped over a few men to reach Bobby. The soldier wasn't moving.

"Bobby," I whispered. "Are you all right?" I pressed on his neck. No pulse. "Bobby, come on," I urged, but I knew it was too late. His skin was cold, and his heart was dead in his chest. "God's bones."

A few moments later, Beth was at my side.

"There will be more coming in soon," she said, wiping sweat from her forehead. "Let's take as many out as we can."

She seemed so old just then; she was only a few years older than me as far as I could tell, but she looked wise and worn-out. There was something different about her these last few days: she held her head higher than before and her shoulders back. It was as if she had grown fifteen years in less than a week. It must have had something to do with this war; she had been here for some months already, it was true, but until now, this had not seemed so monumental. When the shots were fired at Sumter, we thought we could send a few men marching down to Richmond to stamp this out just like any other rebellion. Now, we knew it was not so.

It took careful maneuvering to drag the bodies out. We had to carry them one at a time, but even then it was hard to see who and what we were stepping over, and I had to make more than a few apologies to men on the ground after accidentally kicking them. We did manage to clear some room, though. I left Bobby on the front porch, placing him down carefully and pressing my hand to the spot on my chest where I was keeping his ring. A considerable pile of bodies rested in the front now. I wished it were easier to take them out back so we didn't have to leave them ominously for the injured men to see as they entered.

Beth and I both returned to our patients, and whenever we had a free moment, we would try to carry another body out, but we didn't often. Bullet to the leg, bayonet to the side, even a bullet through the ear—just grazing the side of his head—for one man. What a fated shot. I had treated Joshua's scraped knees, but the woman I was even yesterday would have fainted at some of these sights. Today, I didn't have the time, but that didn't stop me from feeling mightily nauseated. I just ignored it.

The surgeon came over quite a time later.

"Shattered bone," I said, gesturing to the spot on the patient's leg.

He inspected it for a few minutes, and I could see the anxiety in the patient's eyes.

"Madam," the surgeon instructed me patronizingly as if I had committed a crime by not following some unspoken instruction of his. "Please fetch the chloroform."

The patient groaned, and my heart dropped. But, I knew it might save his life.

It wasn't hard to press the cloth over the man's mouth. If I held it long enough, he would pass out, but I didn't know if the surgeon would wait that long. I had seen men go into amputations in a half-conscious state; it was a terrible sight. After a few minutes, the surgeon seemed satisfied.

He simply said, "Make sure he doesn't move."

It was an awful thing. It was an awful, awful thing. It didn't take long—it was over in minutes—and the soldier *was* unconscious for it, thank the Lord, but there was a fraction of a second when I panicked and thought, *"I can't do this."*

The surgeon gave me an odd look and left me to dispose off the amputated limb while he fixed up the patient. I picked up the bloody thing, and my nose pinched to touch it. It was like a rat; it wouldn't hurt me, I knew it wouldn't, but by God, it was difficult not to panic and cast it away from myself.

Outside the window, I knew, was where I was supposed to put the thing, but I hadn't actually assisted an amputation yet, so I hadn't done this before. I reached out to the already-open back window and, God's bones, it was horrific. I saw a pile of limbs stacked up like corpses, and the stench was unbearable. I felt as if I was going to faint. If I felt much worse than this, I would have to ask one of the other nurses if they had a smelling salt.

Some time later, maybe an hour, I was just finishing the bandages on a man that looked far too old to be here when one of the other nurses rushed in.

"Make room! Make room!" she cried, and behind her, people were shuffling in with stretchers, men were limping into the room, and although it was not clear what had happened, I knew one thing for sure: it was going to be utter chaos. We, nurses, leaped from our tasks and began scrounging for more space, forcing men to scoot closer together and asking some if they could move outside. They were always gracious about it, but some of the men who moved were obviously not strong enough for the task—we let them lean on us while they limped to the porch, where they would sit upright on legs they could not use.

We were directing the newly arrived into cramped spaces when I had a sudden vision, a sudden thought that if there were so many wounded—God's bones, so many dying—what if Joshua was one of them? What if he was here in this hospital, or somewhere else on the battlefield, bleeding a river, and I would never know until too late? What if I couldn't ever find him?

I pressed a hand to my chest and dismissed it. I couldn't even consider such things, not at this moment. Not now.

After the rush, it was wound after wound, and soon I found myself saddled with an abundance of requests: *Write to my sister, will you? Please tell my wife what's happened. Here, take this to my mother.* I couldn't possibly remember them all, but I tried.

"Those goddamn Rebels," one man gasped. "If I go out this way, I hope you'll let me go out there with a gun and blow as many of their brains out as I can before I drop dead."

I didn't know how to respond to that.

"God, don't let them take my arm," another pleaded. "How am I supposed to work crops with only one arm? Tell me that, madam. What am I supposed to do without my arm?"

I didn't know what to say to him, either.

In late afternoon—or at least it must have been that time, but I wasn't sure—a soldier named Henry entered the house with visible bloodstains on his uniform, but he did not seem injured.

"Sir! Are you all right?"

"We've got to go, madam."

"What?"

"Take as many as you can. There're ambulances outside. The Rebels have won. We must flee."

"But they wouldn't come here!"

"We're all retreating. If you don't come with us, you might lose us."

"Okay." I rubbed my forehead and took a deep breath. "Okay. But will you help us, sir?"

He nodded, *Of course*. So everybody who was able to stand on their two feet set to work. With great effort, we were able to load all of the men into the ambulances—not comfortably, but at least they were all there—and Henry spoke to the steward.

"We'll have to cut through just beside the battlefield."

"Can't we make a detour? Such sights would certainly disturb the fine ladies who are coming with us."

I bit my lip. It was true, at least partly, but I hated to admit it.

"We could," Henry said, "but we risk losing the rest of the soldiers. We'd be able to find their eventual location no matter what, but I think we can both agree that it would be preferable not to spend all night looking for it. We'd best stay close to the battlefield."

The steward looked nervous.

"We can handle it," one of the nurses assured him, and immediately, I wished I'd spoken up first. "If it's what must be done, we will do it. We'll be fine."

Both men looked around at us. There were more than a dozen nurses, and about half of us were women. Seeing our consensus, the steward shrugged.

"We'll cut through, then. But ladies, be careful. It will be a long walk."

So, to the tune of pained groans from soldiers and the quiet gasps of horrified nurses, we set off.

That night, Beth was absent from our tent. I set out to look for her and found her at the edge of camp, throwing up into the dry grass at our feet.

"Dear, dear!" I cried, frightening her. I trotted to her side and scooped her hair behind her head.

In a few minutes, her horrible retching was done.

"I'm so sorry," she said. *"You have nothing to apologize for,"* I thought.

"The sight of the battlefield has simply made me ill."

The air had grown cold, and Beth shivered. Her excuse was perfectly believable—I had thought many times today that I might throw up, too, after the things we'd seen— but I sensed that she wasn't telling me the truth. Not the whole truth, at least. But what did she have to lie about?

I pressed a hand to her back as we walked back to our tent.

"You're going to be okay," I told her, but I wasn't sure if it was true.

Chapter Three

"Bastards," he said. "The rat bastards."

I shifted uncomfortably. We'd found the soldiers, all right, but the mood at the camp was violently depressing. Me? I couldn't stand to think about it. Joshua was okay; that, at least, was true. I had taken to sewing, writing letters, playing cards, anything to keep my mind off the rest of it. The soldiers seemed to be doing the same—with more curse words, perhaps.

Joshua continued with his complaints, shuffling a deck of cards and distributing them between the two of us for a short game. I truly didn't understand his attitude—he'd wanted to be a part of this war, had he not? Would he really be happier if we won immediately, and it all ended? I knew I would be able to rest easier, but somehow I was not the one letting out a string of foul-mouthedness.

"It's treason, really," he continued, placing a queen into the dry summer grass between us, and this comment, I knew, was not entirely of his own thinking. He was spouting other people's words. "They think they can commit treason against our nation and then they have the audacity to kill our men? It's sick, Cassie. It's sick."

I didn't have a word to say about it. At least he was sitting beside me. "I told you this all was dangerous." It was so tempting to ask him how the battle had been and how close he had come to riding back here in one of the dirty ambulances in front of me. Did he now understand? Did he regret his stupid, naive decision? Likely not, but I wanted to ask all the same. I put down a ten and, since his queen was higher, he took both cards.

He sighed. "It's not about that, Cassie. Don't you get it? It's not about my safety, or yours, or anybody's. We have something bigger to fight for. It's our duty to save this nation. If that means I must suffer a few bullet wounds, lose an arm, even give up my life, then I will do it."

"Technically," I thought bitterly, *"it's not your duty, because you're still underage."*

However, I bit my tongue—he may not be doing this for duty, but there was still a good reason for it, and I had to remember that.

"You've got a spot there."

"What?" he asked.

I pointed to his uniform. On one of the sleeves, there was a spot of red.

"Oh." He touched it and tried faintly to rub it off. "It's just blood."

"I can wash it if you'd like."

He did appear to consider it.

"No, I think I'll keep it." He shrugged. "It's not worth the trouble."

His card finally beat mine, and he scooped an unusually large pile toward himself. After a bit of silence—Joshua was rapidly earning the whole deck for himself, but I was happy to lose this game—Joshua asked, "Did you do many amputations?"

What an odd question.

"The surgeons do it. I did administer the chloroform, though, to knock the boys out. I did that many times."

"What was it like? Being in the hospital?"

I shrugged. If he was going to cross that line, I would cross it, too.

"What was it like in battle?"

"I asked first."

"Well, I'm the oldest, so you should do as I say."

He shoved my shoulder, laughing. "Answer the question!"

"It was gross, and it looked awfully painful. Trust me, it's not something you want to hear much about."

"How long did it take?"

"A few minutes? I was busy trying not to faint."

He rolled his eyes. "You were always so weak-stomached."

"You try it, Joshua. It smelled awful."

My brother laughed, probably at me.

I said, "Now it's your turn."

He had the whole deck of cards now, and he raised his eyebrows: *Another game?* I shrugged, nodded, and he began to speak as he distributed the cards.

"It was fine," he said, and I was tempted to heckle him, to make him explain, but I sensed that he just couldn't find the right words. Even if he knew how to explain, I might never get a clear answer from him.

We played a few more card games with sparse conversation. It seemed that anything we might have desired to say was unspeakable.

Later that night, when I arrived in the tent, Beth wasn't there.

"Beth?" I called and asked the others if they'd seen her. Nothing.

Now, I didn't know her well, but there was a gnawing feeling in my stomach. She could be with Nicholas; maybe she was staying in his tent. But with all the other soldiers there, it wouldn't be allowed.

Still, I searched for Nicholas, and when I managed to find him, his response was, "Beth? She left a quarter of an hour ago. Are you sure she's not in your tent?"

I was very, very sure. And I also knew that something was wrong. Something was terribly wrong.

Deep into the forest I went, calling her name. I didn't know why she would be here, but a thorough search of the camp had proved nothing, and it was worth a try, at least. She wouldn't have gone too far, would she? I dearly hoped not.

"Beth?" I called again. Then I heard it, ever so quiet: a small rustling sound. "Beth."

A sniffle. Or at least that was what I thought I heard.

"Beth!"

Finally, I reached her. She was sitting against a tree, and when I shined my lantern on her, she looked oddly calm. I had, for some reason, expected to find her in hysterics.

"Cassie, I need you to leave."

Her face was stoic, and her words were firm.

"When did she learn my name?" I thought.

"What are you doing here?"

"Nothing of concern. I'll be back to camp in half of an hour." She gulped but not fearfully. "Probably."

I saw a small bottle in her hand and inched closer.

"Beth, what are you *doing*?"

It looked like a vial of the ointment we used to treat cuts. If she'd only taken one bottle, it certainly wouldn't be noticed, but why would she come all the way out here just to treat a cut? Perhaps it was in a rather private area, but she didn't seem to have any gauze. No, this wasn't a cut.

"Cassie, really," she said, moving to stand up, but she apparently decided against it. "You should go. I'm just taking care of something."

"What exactly is that going to take care of?" I gestured to the bottle, and she closed her hand around it evasively.

"It's nothing. Please go. Please."

"I can't leave you out here by yourself. What are you doing with that thing? I can help you treat a cut. You don't need to come out here and hide."

"It's not for a cut." Despite her appearance of disinterest, I could sense fear or guilt. Maybe both.

"What, are you going to drink it?"

Silence.

"Why would you drink it?"

Silence.

"It really shouldn't do anything. I heard somewhere that it—

well, I just wanted to see what would happen."

"What does it do?"

"Nothing. I just wanted to try it."

I stepped closer and grabbed her hand, the one that held the bottle.

"*What does it do*?"

"It's none of your business!" She shook free. "Why are you doing this?"

"Because I care about you, and for all we know," I said as I breathed, "that thing can kill you."

"It won't kill me," she swore resolutely.

And then I realized: It won't kill *me*.

Oh, God. How had I not seen this?

She wouldn't. Would she? She had spoken of *wanting* a child. Why would she take it all away now? Bad timing, sure, but was there ever good timing? Even in peace, crops failed and typhus struck; if she waited for a *good time*, her womb would be perpetually empty.

"Beth, are you—"

"Don't say it. I don't want to talk about it. Just leave me alone, Cassie."

I took a deep breath. "Beth, you can't do this."

"It's my only chance!"

She began to panic as I tried to wrench the bottle from her grasp.

"Stop!" she cried. "Cassie, you don't understand!"

"Don't I?"

I didn't know why I was so angry. It wasn't really my business, was it? But someone had to do something. Beth *couldn't* do this.

"This might just be the stupidest thing you've ever tried."

Her eyes sparked with rage.

"Do you think I *want* to do this? You don't think I would rather keep it? Because I would, Cassie. I would. But I don't know what

I'm going to do now. I can't have a baby here! I can't go home, either. What would you have me do?"

"I want you to stop and think."

She lifted her chin, and her lips wobbled, but her gaze was firm.

"Do you want a child?" I asked. "It will be hard, I know, but there are people who can help you. This will pass, Beth, all of this will pass, and it might seem difficult now, but think about when this is over. Will you regret what you've given up?"

She was like a ghost, her eyes dark and searching. I wished we were not in such darkness. There was little light from my lantern, and if I were to blow it out, we would be in near-complete blackness, guided only by a very faint light from the distant camp. I was not afraid of the dark, but I longed to be back at the camp, in a warm tent—warm, of course, being a relative word—with the other nurses, sweaty and snoring as they may have been. I needed that bottle out of Beth's hands. I knew she wasn't unstable, only desperate, but it made me uneasy to see her pale hands grasping it so tightly all the same. She clutched it like it was an elixir, like it would bring her life, but I knew that there were no answers at the bottom of a bottle. Not any bottle, but especially not this one.

Beth said, "If something happens to Nicholas, I will have to raise it alone."

"Is it not true also that if something happens to Nicholas, this child is the last thing you will have of him?"

She seemed to consider that. It had already run through her mind, I was sure, and maybe she had dismissed it, but it was a valid truth. If she truly loved her husband, would she not want to keep this last part of him?

"If it is so, I cannot use a child to try to revive him. I cannot bear the thought of doing this without him—I cannot bear it, Cassie, do you understand?"

I thought of the news that Joshua had enlisted, and I did

understand, at least somewhat: I knew that I could not stand to be helpless to save my brother, just as she could not bear to raise a child if her husband was not there beside her. I would have felt differently, but I understood. And yet, I knew that I could not stand to let her do this. I could not stand to watch her destroy this child.

"Would he want this?" I asked. "If he knew, would he accept this?"

Beth blinked. "It doesn't matter because he won't."

"I can't let you do this."

"Cassie, please go."

It was a final plea, the last straw. She was going to do this, no matter what I said.

So, in the quickest of movements, I wrenched the bottle from her hands, dropped it on the ground, and smashed it with my foot.

Immediately, I felt a jolt of regret. Who was I to make this decision for her? If it had been me, I would have been furious at the person who tried to make this choice for me. I could not control her life, and I could not save her from sin. She looked at me with the narrowest of eyes, and hate spilled out almost like teardrops, visible on the planes of her face. I waited for her to spit in my face, as Joshua had so many days ago, or strike me across the cheek. Either way, I would have accepted it without blame, but I could not bring myself to regret preventing this murder.

She stormed away. I stood in the wake of her kicked-up dust, and victory surged in my chest.

"I could not save my brother, Beth," I thought, *"but at least I saved you."*

I lifted my skirt off the ground as I made my way to the hospital tent. Last night I had hardly slept, wracked with guilt but somehow not regret. I had made the right decision, I concluded, but I wished

I did not have to be the one to do it. If only Beth had done it herself. The other nurse was explicitly refusing to speak to me, which wasn't noticeable in a camp of such size as ours, but it still stung. Of course, she would not look at me for days, that was to be expected, but I had still fostered a shred of hope that she'd had some sort of epiphany after she stormed off. She might try to make a grab for another ointment bottle, and it was uncertain whether I would be able to catch her in the act again.

Two men were standing guard in front of the tent. It really was noble of them, I thought, for they weren't under orders to do it, but the privates had all decided to take shifts. What exactly they were guarding against, I wasn't sure. Another run-in with the Rebels wasn't likely to happen during the night, and even traitors like them wouldn't have the nerve to harm the infirm. Or would they?

"G'day, ma'am." One of the guards tipped his hat at me. "Checking in on the men?"

I considered replying sarcastically, something like *No, I'm looking for a dance partner*, but he was only being friendly.

"I am, sir."

"Be careful. There's a patient in there—well, he's quite all right now, but when he starts up, he goes on yelling and yelling, *'There's a storm coming, mark my words! A right storm!'* It's not too bad at first, but it's difficult to listen for very long." There was a double row of buttons on his coat. He was an officer, then, perhaps not a high-ranking one, but an officer all the same.

I replied with a quick thanks before entering the tent. There are fewer patients now. They've gotten out of here, one way or the other, and now they can all fit into one tent. There's not a lot of room, and they could easily fill up two if we had the provisions for that, but we didn't.

There were two nurses inside already. Just before me, one was cleaning a cut with the ointment. God's bones, the ointment. The mere sight of it turned my stomach. I couldn't imagine drinking that: it probably tasted worse than the wrong end of a donkey, and for all anyone knew, it was lethal.

"Is something troubling you?" the nurse asked sweetly, and I realized I had been staring at her for quite some time.

Her name was Anne, maybe Amy—I knew I'd heard it somewhere. Like most of the nurses, she was rather homely—there was nothing striking about her features, really, and she had a forgettable sort of kindness, the sort that doesn't lend itself to many descriptors.

"No," I replied as if I myself was surprised by the answer. "I'm all right. Is there anything specific you'd like me to do?"

"Well, Johnson over there could use another dressing," she gestured, "And if you have time, there are always some men who want to dictate letters."

Johnson had a shadow of a beard on his cheeks. It was as if he had been clean-shaven, but in the few days that he had been bedridden, it had fallen to neglect.

"Johnson is his first name?"

She shrugged.

"Might be his last name. That was what he told us to call him."

I grabbed the ointment and gauze and approached him politely.

"How easygoing I am now," I thought, *"how friendly. Not the monster that Beth must believe me to be."*

Johnson beamed when I reached his bedside.

"So, Johnson," I smiled as I said, immediately spotting the injury on his left arm and preparing to replace the bandage. "How are you feeling?"

His voice was like sandpaper, and I realized he looked familiar. I'd seen him about the camp before, most likely.

"Just dandy, madam."

It sounded sarcastic, but I couldn't be sure.

When I was finished with the bandage, he grabbed my arm with his good one.

"You're an angel," he said, sincerely, for certain.

How surprising! Maybe if someone had praised me this way during the battle when we, nurses, were bustling about like mad people, trying to make room and bandage legs and pour whiskey for the amputations, I would understand the sentiment. But an angel now, here, just wrapping bandages and chatting with the other nurses? He was surely referring to the battle when we worked dawn to dusk with hardly a minute of rest.

"I only do God's work, sir. I would call you the same for your sacrifices."

He shook his head. "Mine are hardly as selfless as yours. You can never know how much."

I smiled, flattered and somewhat bewildered.

"I'm afraid I don't quite understand, sir."

Johnson's gaze was clear and overwhelmingly grateful. "You saved my life."

I laughed, more of a sound of shock than anything.

"The best I've done so far is to bandage wounds, sir. I'm not sure you would call that 'lifesaving.'"

"It saved my life," he said as if it were that simple.

As if a single bandage was life or death.

A ring glinted on his finger.

"Married," I thought, although he did look young.

I had given Bobby's ring to the company captain, trusting him to send it where it belonged, but a jolt of panic surged through me.

"What if it doesn't arrive? What if the captain forgot to send it? How will his wife—"

As I tied the last knot, the patient thanked me earnestly. I felt uneasy, and I didn't know why.

I did the rounds, mostly re-bandaging. At one point, the second nurse, Eleanor, started to make conversation. It drifted in and out of my head, trite observations that were hard to pay attention to, but then she asked, "Do you know what is bothering Beth? She seems awfully gloomy this morning."

My throat caught.

"Well," I began, heading toward the stack of pen and paper, "perhaps she's simply not feeling well."

"That could be the situation," she responded as if disappointed with the answer. "Something just feels unusual. Don't you think so? I think there's something wrong with her."

"Is it really that noticeable?" I gulped.

There were so many of us that the mood of a single nurse shouldn't be of much concern to the rest of us unless we were close. These ladies, I knew, were not very close with Beth.

"Well, she and I usually talk a little during breakfast, and this morning, she refused to say a single word. I just thought, since you two seem to know each other so well that you would know if something's wrong. Or you'd like to, at the very least."

She and Beth did talk during breakfast, I supposed, but it wasn't a daily occurrence. Eleanor was just fishing for information to entertain herself.

"She told me she's been feeling sick. I'm sure she's just receiving the worst of it at the moment. Would you agree?"

"Yes, yes," Eleanor said, and her tone was either delightfully sincere or deceitfully sarcastic. "I think you're correct."

The room was filled with the quiet buzz of the infirm making short conversation. Those who weren't unconscious or insane usually engaged in cheerful small talk: predictions about the war, hopeful comments about their conditions, even awful jokes. Nobody talked about the battle. It was as if it'd never happened, as if they'd gone from living in perfect health with their families to lying in an army hospital bed with holes in their arms by some unfortunate accident. I was beginning to understand why Joshua hadn't talked to me about it; besides not wanting to talk to me, which I'm sure was part of it, he just couldn't.

A breeze whooshed in. Standing near the tent flaps were two

men with single-row buttons on their coats.

"We're very sorry, ladies. Do we overwhelm you?" one asked.

The tent was a little crowded, but I didn't mind much, and nobody else said a word, so the men made their way to one of the injured.

"John, how are you feeling?" one of them greeted him.

They didn't seem to care whether anyone heard them, but nevertheless, I turned back to my patient to disguise my eavesdropping.

"Storm," John mumbled. "There's a storm coming."

"What are you talking about?"

"There's a storm coming! It's coming here. It's going to destroy us."

"What storm? Who told you about a storm?"

"There's a storm. There's a storm coming."

And so it continued, and periodically, his voice would rise to a near screech. He was the one the guards outside had warned me about. I understood what they meant when they said it was annoying. It was unnerving, too; it gave me gooseflesh.

"Should I tend to him?" I thought.

We had not received instructions regarding matters such as this.

"Just let him be as he is," Eleanor advised. "He'll get over it eventually."

"Are we not to treat him?"

She laughed. "What would we do for the man? There's no medicine for it."

"There's a storm coming! It's coming for all of us!" his mumbling continued.

The soldiers who had come to visit him looked ready to take leave. Apparently, they had not expected him to act in such a manner.

"No," Eleanor said as his screeches grew louder, "the only

thing to do is to wait for it to pass."

And so, as I made my way around writing letters for the soldiers, that was what we did. We waited for it to pass.

I didn't see Georgeanna fall in step beside me so much as feel her. Every afternoon we were given a break and allowed to go on walks. More often than not those walks led us to the camp—or at least for me, to visit Joshua—but the men were doing drills at this hour, so I had decided to simply wander about the trees, perhaps stumbling upon the stream that I was sure was nearby.

"I hope you don't mind my company," Georgeanna said, taking a square of hardtack from her pack. "I'm a bit lonely these days, and since I saw you alone, I thought I would join you."

"It's quite all right," I remarked. "I could use some company, too.

"You look very glum," Georgeanna remarked, and as much as I was unwilling to talk about it, I was glad someone, at least, had noticed.

"It's nothing, really."

I poked a stick into the crackling fire before us. When it was aflame, I threw it in. "I'm simply worrying about my brother. He's a soldier, though not quite of age, and we both came here a few months ago thinking this would be a sure way to feed ourselves, but sometimes I think I have made a mistake in letting Joshua put his life in danger."

Georgeanna coughed.

"Well, I don't have the problem that you do, but I believe I understand it somewhat. What would you both have done if you had not come here?"

I shrugged.

"We could have gone to Springfield and worked in a factory.

Or, I could have a husband somehow and let Joshua live with us until he could make a living for himself. I'm not sure. But I would find a way to take care of him."

"He's a man now, though, isn't he?"

No. But I supposed that, in a way, he was.

"And would you really rather work in a factory than here? I come from New York, and I have met many people who do it. It's not something you ever want."

"But he's risking his life here."

"He knows that, though, doesn't he? It's worth it. Battle is awful, but the pay is good, and there's much more time to relax. There's an honor in it, too. When your brother comes back home, he will be a hero."

"If he *does* come back home."

Georgeanna patted my arm.

"Now," she said, "how do you expect to support your brother with an attitude like that? Have some faith. God will see us all through this."

"Yes," I chuckled, "I suppose He will."

The words tasted hollow.

Chapter Four

Joshua had always been a mischievous child. That was what I was thinking as I traipsed into the hospital next morning. I couldn't explain why that thought had come to mind, but there I was, face to face with the infirm men, and I couldn't get the image of my brother as a little boy out of my head. Dark, curly hair. Innocent blue eyes. The way he'd call me "Caddy" before he could pronounce the letter *S*. The mud pies he would make with his chubby little hands and then smile his big wide smile as he showed me the completed ones. I wasn't much older than him—not even two years, in fact—but he always looked up to me, he always did.

At the end of the day, when night fell, the first whispers of a storm began.

"It's going to be a long night," I heard one of the soldiers outside muse. "What do you think, Johnny?"

"Let's hope we can keep our hats on."

Some of the soldiers urged me to return to my tent with the other nurses. Beth was staying, though, and I knew it would be smarter just to leave her, but I didn't. I could make it look like my decision to stay had nothing to do with her. She might even believe me.

So we waited out the storm.

It was a raucous thing, howling wind and pouring rain. Nothing I hadn't seen before, but I'd always been at home when it happened. Experiencing a storm inside a cabin, however weak it may have been, was a lot different than watching tent flaps whipping violently and wondering if it would eventually be wholly knocked down.

I wondered how the other soldiers were. Was Joshua okay? It was mighty cold, and I knew most of the men were well-clothed for it, but I still wondered.

A small voice, one that was not mine, said, *"He's fine."*

"Goddamn," one of the patients muttered. "If it gets any windier, we might be able to start flying."

"I don't think that's how flying works, Jerry." One of the other men chuckled. "Unless you're talking about flying straight into a tree."

"Oh, it sure is how it works. Isn't it? The windier it is, the easier it becomes for the birds to fly."

Jerry's commentator looked entirely convinced otherwise but said nothing. I stifled a small laugh.

Beth looked sideways toward us. She was kneeling at the far end of the tent, less than three paces away, and her face revealed no expression. I wondered if she had told Nicholas about the child. Or had she used the ointment successfully this time? My stomach churned at the thought.

Most of the men with us were sitting up and chatting gaily, but one, in particular, just lay there. If I recalled correctly, he had typhus; it was imperative that he not get wet.

"Ah," came a groan as a particularly ferocious gust of wind blew the tent every way.

"The only thing that would make this better is some cold gruel." He laughed.

Thus we sat for hours more, waiting for the storm to end and leave us in peace, but it only grew stronger. Soon, we were clutching our clothes as the wind howled curses and pushed roughly against the tent.

"God's bones," I thought, "what if the tent is knocked over?"

I instinctively opened my mouth to speak to Beth about it before remembering myself.

Not a quarter of an hour later, my question was answered. Those of us who could sit up had begun a mild game of cards, although, any speaking was inaudible now. A sudden gust of wind came whooshing by, and for a single second, I felt as if it would swipe my head clean off. The guards, who had joined us inside to avoid getting their clothes soaking wet, looked up from their cards.

"We have to get Owen somewhere safe," one said, gesturing to the typhus-ridden patient who was groaning and attempting to prop himself up on his elbows, "now."

Beth and I looked at each other, and though her eyes were cold and unforgiving, we understood—at least somewhat—what we needed to do.

As the guards wrapped an arm each of Owen's around their soldiers, Beth and I followed them out of the tent. The stretchers were back at the nurses' tents, and they wouldn't have been of any use to us now anyhow.

"There's a house at the top of the hill," one said, pointing. "We'll need Godspeed."

So they went, clambering up the hill as the wind slapped them harder than alcohol-imbued hands, and Beth and I ran ahead as best we could to alert the home's owner of our arrival. At the top of the hill, we began to pant horribly. I rapped on the door.

No response.

"We have a dying man here!" I shouted as the guards joined us at the peak. "I will allow three seconds before I knock this door down!"

In periphery, I saw the guards glance at each other, and it occurred to me that it would be unusual for a lady like me to kick down a door. No matter. It was life or death now, and I would do it.

"I can't let you in!" we heard from inside.

"A man is dying!" I screeched, struggling to be heard over the storm. "I will break it down."

The door opened and revealed an old man, pale-faced and annoyed, but his expression turned to concern when he saw Owen.

He quickly shuffled aside to let us through, saying, "My apologies. I did not hear you until now."

His eyes were still fixed on our near-unconscious patient,

whose clothes were soaked through.

"There's a couch in the living room. Let me get some blankets."

He was gone only a few seconds and returned just as we were placing Owen on the couch. Beth and I stepped out of the room while someone helped to change his clothes into dry clothes and wrapped him in blankets. I almost expected Beth to make her normal conversation, to say something like, 'Oh, I do hope he's okay.' I think she considered it, too, but she let me suffer in heavy silence. Her pregnancy was showing, I noticed, but just a bit. Only someone who knew about it would be able to see. So she hadn't committed murder after all.

After a long enough period of pointed stares, we were allowed back into the room. I lifted my skirt as we walked, hoping it wouldn't drip water onto the ground, but despite my efforts, a trail of droplets was left in my wake. I longed to be in dry clothes and wished my hair at least had stayed dry—in less than an hour, it would be tremendously frizzy. I knew this from experience. Joshua used to laugh at it to the point where I would refuse to take a single step outside until I knew it was completely dry just to avoid his mockery. That didn't last long, though; it would often drizzle on days we had to help with the crops, and Joshua was forced to promise not to say a word. I often did see him smirking, though. I hadn't really cared that he laughed, but when the simple act of asking him to stop was not a deterrent, I promised myself I would not back down. I didn't expect it to go that far.

"Typhus," I heard the guard named Ashley explain to our host. "With his fever, I don't know how bad the rain was for him."

Our host hummed a sympathetic sound.

"We'll just have to wait, then."

All three of the men, the host and our two guards, glanced at Beth and me.

"Do you have any ointments?" I asked. "For the rash."

Ashley glanced at Owen. He did indeed have a rash on his neck and lower face, probably on his arms, too. The ill man burst into a fit of dry coughs that was painful to our ears.

"I'll see what I can find in the cabinet. Do you need anything else?"

I shrugged. "Whiskey would be great."

I was thinking that we could use it to ease his pain if needed.

A few moments later, we were supplied with some ointment and the whiskey, and Owen was still coughing horribly. By his bedside now, I studied the small bottle of salve to discern what it was. I couldn't even read the label.

"Do you know what this is?"

Our host sighed.

"God help me if I remember. My wife, God rest her soul, used it to clear up rashes, so it must be helpful to you."

Well, it was worth a try, wasn't it? I rubbed some of it onto my finger, and as the biting smell wafted to my nose, I struggled not to glance at Beth, who was sitting next to me, her attitude unreadable, and she was holding the whiskey. To *drink* something like this ointment? God, I had to stop thinking about it.

"Owen?" I asked as I began to rub the substance onto his neck. "Owen? Can you say something? How are you feeling?"

"Cold," he croaked. "I'm cold."

I pulled the blanket up as much as I could, aware of everyone's alert attention.

"Are there more blankets?" I asked nobody in particular.

The host—John, I heard the guard Ashley call him—shook his head.

"That's every blanket in the house."

"Well, is there anything else? Old clothes, towels, anything?"

Beth patted my shoulder sympathetically. "He's got dry clothes and blankets. There's nothing more we can do about it."

"He says he's still cold. We have to try, don't we?"

Just then the coughing gained momentum such that he was hardly breathing.

"God's bones," I whispered.

Everybody in the room looked at each other, and we were all thinking the same thing.

"Let us pray," Ashley said.

We had no priest, we had no rites, but maybe if the four of us together prayed hard enough, that could be forgiven. Owen could confess his last sins to God instead of a man.

I held his hand through the prayer, squeezing periodically to see if he was still with us.

Ashley spoke beautifully, "Dear Lord in Heaven, we pray for Owen that You will keep him with us if that is Your will, or otherwise take him peacefully to Your side. We pray that You will watch over him and grant him the strength to come back to us. Every breath of his is precious to us now, Lord, and if there is a path we must take to keep him here, we beg that You show it to us or grant us the wisdom to see it ourselves. And if he must go, God, then we pray that he will do so in peace and comfort and that You will watch over him every second."

I squeezed Owen's hand, and this time, he did not squeeze back; there was no pulse.

"John," I whispered. "He's gone."

Beth pressed a hand to her mouth. She was at his feet, and the men were on the other side of the sofa, leaning over just a bit to see the afflicted. All was quiet.

"Lord, watch over him," I prayed, and I was certain the others were doing the same.

It was eerily silent. The storm had ceased, and it seemed that we were all holding our breaths.

"Well, bless the poor boy," John said.

A small sob escaped from Beth's lips.

We could do nothing with the body until morning. We would

take it down to the camp then, Ashley had determined, and the captain would determine how he would be buried or if he would be buried. Many soldiers died in battle and never saw a proper grave for there were so many dying all at once. If he was lucky, his mama would come down when she received the news and give him a good and proper burial, but I'd never seen it happen. Sometimes the Southern women would come out from the towns and take care of the bodies, but if they did, it was with fiery eyes and curled-up lips; they were reluctant to take care of any but their own. So none of us knew what the captain would have us do with the body of Owen.

As for slumber—and we didn't get much of it that night—John offered a single spare room, which the soldiers graciously gifted to Beth and me, while they rested on the living room floor. How they would manage to sleep with the corpse still untouched on the sofa in that same room I didn't understand. They were probably accustomed to such things, though, now. Beth and I followed John up the stairs, and when he gestured toward the guest room, and we bid him good night, I followed her inside.

The bed was hardly large enough for both of us.

"I'll sleep on the floor," I offered, but as the bed had already been almost stripped because the blankets had been given to Owen, and nobody had the mind or the heart to remove them, there wasn't an extra blanket for me.

Beth shook her head. Her eyes were red-rimmed, but she showed no more signs of grief nor even of solemnity—she looked entirely drained of emotion. It was a common expression for her these days, or at least she always bore it whenever I looked her way.

I was nervous as I climbed into bed beside her. I didn't expect to get much sleep at all after everything that had happened, and I wondered if I was alone in that. Beth was turned the other way, so as I lay awake trying to forget the exact second when I felt Owen's pulse go dry, I was unsure whether she was awake, too, having similar thoughts.

Finally, when I was convinced she must be asleep, I whispered, "I'm sorry."

I didn't know what I was sorry for, exactly. Was I sorry for smashing that bottle? Not really. But I was sorry for the grief it caused her, and I was sorry for her tears tonight.

She shifted, and I thought she might be awake.

I thought she might respond by saying, *"It's all right, Cassie."* Or, *"I now realize how great my sin was, and I will never try such a horrible thing again."*

Instead, she sighed and drifted to sleep.

The men had wanted to bury the body properly, but it wasn't going to be that way: the camp was in disarray after the storm, and their labor was much needed. So they carried the body to the edge of the battlefield and left it there among the others. Owen would receive as good a burial as the other soldiers, that was to say, probably none. Maybe some townsfolk would eventually come out to bury the bodies to get rid of the smell, but that was likely the best we could hope for. We didn't have time to bury everyone; we had to keep moving.

So Beth and I were walking down the hill back to camp when I asked, "Have you told Nicholas yet?"

She stiffened.

"No," she said shortly and provided no detail.

Fine, then. That was fine.

"I hope I have not ruined our friendship with my actions that night," I said, quietly enough that the others would not hear us though they, of course, would have no idea what we were talking about anyway.

"I dare not apologize for them, but I wish I had not been forced to do what I did."

Her sigh sounded derisive, and I thought she might begin to yell at me or, worse, ignore me.

"It's funny," she said. "I wish you hadn't done it, but I think it's better that you did."

"I told you it would turn out fine," I replied with relief, intending to be comforting.

"As if you would know. You're just naive, you know. You mean well, but you know nothing."

How amusing. Had she been there when Ma was lowered into her grave—the last time I saw the light in my father's eyes? Had she been there when Joshua had a fever and when I stopped cooking and cleaning in order to revive him, and I didn't eat for three days? I was young, yes, and I had not seen as much as some, but I very much felt like I had seen more than enough to not be called "naïve."

"You know nothing about me."

"And if you'd known anything about me, you wouldn't have done what you did."

I sighed. "Well, I'm sorry, all right? I'm sorry if it hurt you, but I don't regret it. I know it was right."

She snorted. "Only a fool would be so certain."

Beth shook her head softly, light curls bouncing on her shoulder.

"I was desperate, Cassie. I was desperate. I *am* desperate. Maybe God intends for me to have this child," she said those last words quietly, likely not wishing them to be overheard, "but I don't know what I'm going to do."

"I'm sorry," I thought.

I wanted to say it, but it felt like such an empty sentiment—I was sure it would sound like I didn't really mean it. But I had nothing else to say. So we sat in silence for a short while, before

Beth rose, sighed as if she had expected better from me, and left my side.

At mid-afternoon, two men were dragged into the hospital with bloody welts on their bare backs, heads down, groaning in pain. A few nurses scurried in after them, laying them down on their stomachs.

"What happened?" I asked Georgeanna, who had just come from outside.

"They got in some argument, the big one gave the boy a licking, and Captain had them both whipped."

On a cot a few feet away, the one who was built like a wine barrel—obviously the one who had given the beating, not taken it—growled as a nurse tried to dab at his welts with a cloth. "Are you trying to kill me, woman?"

"If you want me to treat your wounds, you must sit still and bear the pain a little longer," she replied calmly.

I turned back to Georgeanna. "Why would Captain have them both whipped?"

She looked at me oddly as if she was deeply surprised that I hadn't already understood.

"That's how things work around here. They both argued, so they both got whipped. Captain's not going to sit and dwell on who did the worse deed."

"Well, if one has a face full of bruises and one doesn't, shouldn't it be obvious who is at fault?"

Georgeanna shook her head. "But the boy could have been the one who started the argument."

"The boy" was just in front of us, groaning quietly as someone treated his wounds. I stepped forward to help, though there was little for an extra nurse to do, and noticed that his sand-colored hair was eerily similar to my brother's. And the birthmark on his neck—

"Oh my God," I muttered.

His nurse, apparently having heard, glanced up at me questioningly.

"May I take your work here?"

She frowned. "Why would you want to do that?"

I shrugged. "You've been working a while. You're in need of a break, don't you think?"

It was a complete fib; I truly had no idea how long she'd been working. But she reacted like a dog after a tossed bone.

"I think you're completely right, thank you for noticing."

She handed me the cloth and grinned as she scampered off.

I used the cloth to dab at the wounds.

"Joshua," I said quietly. "What have you done?"

He craned his neck a little. "Cassie?" He pressed his face into the cot and groaned. "It wasn't my fault."

"I suppose you were possessed, then, to start an argument with that man over there."

"He started it, I swear, Cassie! He was talking about how this war is for fools and we shouldn't be giving up our lives for negroes and everyone who calls us heroes is out of their mind. It was just disrespectful! We work so hard to be here, we risk our lives, and he thinks that we're idiots who should simply let the traitors abandon our Union? It is disgraceful!"

Truthfully, I cringed a little. Did he really think this was why we were here? "I know it's frustrating, but you *can't* get in fights like this. If you get in any more trouble, it will be bad for both of us."

He sighed. "This is more important than you or me, Cassie."

I chuckled. "But if you get yourself kicked out, what use can you be?"

He was silent for a while.

"It wasn't my fault, really," he said finally, and his words were somewhat muffled by the pillow he was pressing the side of his face into. "Bastard didn't know what he was talking about. He kept saying that this is all nonsense, that the Union has turned into nigger-lovers, and everybody who fights for it is a nigger-lover, too. Just lies! If you'd been there, Cassie, you would have punched him, too."

I was entirely certain that I would *not* have punched him, too, but I let it go, especially because Joshua's aggressor was *right there*, a few cots over.

"Joshua!" I hissed. "You've got to be careful about what you say."

It wasn't as if the fellow would do anything about it, at least not at the moment, but it wasn't a good idea to make any more trouble.

"What?" he snorted. "You think I care if he hears me? He's a right bastard. With the things he's saying, it's a wonder they don't check his coat for papers."

"The man was highly unlikely to be a spy if he was acting openly mutinous," I thought. *"Wouldn't he try to blend in?"*

"Watch it, you little cockroach," the man groused.

I rubbed my forehead with my hand.

"God's bones, Joshua," I hissed. "Shut up and let me do this. Don't you dare make any more trouble."

"*God's bones, Joshua,*" he mimicked, and I was so close to striking him, welts and all.

"Joshua. . ." I hissed, and he mimicked me again.

"That's it," I thought and threw down the towel I had been treating him with. "Fine. Find someone else to do this."

As I stormed out, he called, "Not a problem!"

I bit my lip and held back tears.

An hour later, Georgeanna found me sitting by the creek with my back propped up against a tree. I wasn't doing anything, not even crying, just staring out into the water. She sat next to me, and I was thinking, *"What are you doing here? How did you find me?"* but I didn't have the voice to ask.

She bumped her shoulder in a consoling way against mine.

"It will all pass in time."

I shuddered at the cold. Of course, it would pass, wouldn't it? I knew that—it didn't change the fact that this was hard. But I knew Georgeanna was trying to console me, so I hummed in agreement and pretended I was going to be okay.

Chapter Five

I was carrying three baskets and a demeanor of utter dread when I heard someone approach me on the dusty country road. Captain had sent me off to gather—or, rather, beg for—supplies from the women in a nearby town, and I was rather not looking forward to confrontations with scorned Southern women. When I asked if I could take one of his pistols with me, he laughed, but it was not a joke. In my communication with him, I had tried not to blame him for the welts on my brother's back, but my fists clenched inadvertently anyhow; I'd tried to ignore it.

"Cassie!" Beth exclaimed and joined me.

She might have called my name several times before I heard this.

"I have news for you."

For a second, she seemed different: it was like glimpsing that bright, reckless girl of a year ago, the girl she was when we first met.

"You must tell me, then."

"I told Nicholas."

I stopped short.

"Congratulations!"

Although it didn't carry much enthusiasm, I truly meant it.

"Yes, he was wonderful. He said if this is what we want, then we should be happy, no matter what. There's no good time for it, Cassie. You were right. My worrying seems so foolish now. I know Nicholas will be fine. I have a sense deep in my gut, and I think it's God telling me that everything will be all right."

"How peculiar," I thought, *"for I have that, too."*

No matter how I worried over Joshua, it was as Beth said: deep in my gut, I knew that God's will was in my favor. Faith. It was faith, and for all that the preachers preached, I realized that I had never felt it before these cold, lonely days of battle; I had never known it truly. Now, my heart settled. God *was* on my side, and on Beth's.

"I feel so much happier now, Cassie. Incomparably happy."

And she looked it, trotting happily beside me.

"And then Captain sent you along with me to ruin your mood?" I joked.

"No! I wanted to come with you. Nicholas is busy, anyhow. He's helping to pack the supplies."

We were due to continue marching tomorrow, which was why I was sent to gather any possible spoils from the vengeful townspeople. We'd done a fair amount of marching in the past few months; this last week, we'd stayed put (perhaps something to do with the storm), but according to a rumor, we were headed for Tennessee. They never told us these things anymore.

It was a long walk before we encountered a single house. The first we found was small and ill-cared for. It was occupied by an old woman who refused to speak to us when we knocked on the door.

"Ma'am!" I shouted. "Ma'am! We are here on account of the United States Army!"

"I won't speak with tyrants!" she shouted. "Leave this place!"

"Ma'am, we are here for a very important reason! Please open the door!"

She swung the door open, frowning. She was like a ghost, paler than a babe, and her face spelled vengeance.

"I asked you to leave. If I have to ask again, I will get my pistol."

"Ma'am, we are here on orders of the United States Army. We need food for our men—"

Both hands moved to her hips.

"The United States Army does not reign here any longer. When our Rebel boys get ahold of you, I hope they shoot every man who wears blue."

She stiffened and said, “Good day to you, ladies,” and slammed the door.

We quickly moved on.

“Are you sure you’re okay with this?” I confirmed, although it wasn’t as if there was anything I could do if she wasn’t.

She could go back, if she wished, but I could not help her because I had to complete my rounds.

“Of course I am. What, you think I would sooner be back at camp?”

I would rather be back at camp, but I sensed that this sentiment would not be appreciated, so I shrugged and led the way to the next house.

“Go away,” we heard before we even knocked on the door. “I won’t help you.”

“Ma’am!” I called. “We are here on the orders of the United States Army!”

“Leave!” the woman cawed, and it sent shivers down my spine.

I banged harder on the door. We may have been driven away by one old crone, but God’s bones, we were going to get food out of somebody.

The door swung open, and I came face-to-face with the barrel of a gun.

“I am not *joking*,” the young woman before me insisted. “I want you to leave.”

Beth stepped forward so she was in better view.

“Please, ma’am, may we just speak to you?”

Perhaps it was Beth’s endearing tone—but the woman softened just a bit. The gun was still pointed at my face, though.

“What do you want?”

“We need food for our men.”

She snorted.

“Men? You mean the *monsters* who killed my boys?”

The gun shifted a bit as if she considered pointing at Beth, but it remained fixed on me. I was getting really nervous.

"They aren't monsters to us, ma'am. They are our boys, our brothers, the fathers of our children."

"You do not know," whispered my aggressor, "what I have lost to the United States Army."

"Whom did you lose?"

The woman seemed taken aback by this question but swiftly responded.

"My husband. Bayonetted on his third day in combat. My brother. Dysentery. And"—her lip trembled—"I haven't heard from my boys in weeks."

"We will send prayers for your sons to come home safely," Beth said sincerely, and I knew that she would follow through with it. She would make me do it, too, I was certain. "And we hope that you will also send prayers for *our* men to come home. We want this war to end as much as you do, my sister." The woman's lip curled at the words *my sister*. "And though our armies are at odds, we are all of the same nation. Your cousin is my cousin, your brother is my brother, do you know? Would you let your brothers starve?"

"They are no family of mine after what they've done," the woman said and dropped the gun. "I have nothing to give you, anyhow. See how I am just skin and bones?"

"Anything would help, ma'am. A lamp, some ink, an old blanket. Anything to help our men."

"I don't want to help your men," the woman said but with less resolve than before.

And she wasn't pointing a gun in my face, so I considered that a change of attitude.

"Then thank you very much for your time, ma'am," said Beth, and we went on our way.

"That was very noble of you to do." I thanked Beth when we were out of the hostile woman's earshot. "You may have just saved my life."

"Oh, she wouldn't have shot you," Beth dismissed as if she knew a thing or two about the matter.

"How do you know that? The gun was right in my face!"

Beth laughed. "Why would she kill you? You were no danger. She just wanted to protect herself."

"It's hard to think like that when there's a gun to your face, that's all I'm going to say."

We reached a fork in the road. Another step, another mile, another house. We would come back empty-handed, I was sure of it, but Beth trudged on alongside me with sweet optimism.

"There's a house," she gestured.

House was a generous term for what she was pointing to. It was more like an ill-maintained hut.

"I don't think we'll find anything there, Beth. Someone like that would sooner be begging from *us*."

"It's worth a try."

She frowned, but when I deliberately failed to turn onto the cottage's path, she stayed by my side.

About an hour we struck gold, so to say. Greeting us was a mansion adorned with two-storied columns and fronted by two enormous oaks. It was a picture of wealth.

"We're stopping here," I declared.

We made our way to the porch where we met a gigantic set of double doors. I slammed the knocker twice, and the sound echoed eerily.

"Beth," I asked, "you didn't happen to bring a pistol with you, did you?"

She laughed. People always thought I was joking about that.

The door creaked open. The woman who faced us was a Southern lady if I ever saw one: a patterned maroon day dress with a full skirt that seemed to take up miles of space, a silver locket at her neck, and a look of quiet but unwavering tenacity.

"What can I do for you?" she intoned in a thick accent, her voice like cream.

"We're here on orders of the United States Army," I replied, waiting for her to be the third woman to threaten with a firearm.

"Oh," she said brightly, and Beth and I both glanced at each other, taken aback. "Well, you may come in. I'll have Mary fix some tea."

"Oh, we cannot stay long, ma'am," I replied. "We're marching tomorrow. We've come to ask for food and supplies."

She frowned in contemplation before her face turned, resolved.

"I'll give you what I can."

"That would be a blessing."

She led us into the parlor, which was unbelievably luxurious, and came back a few minutes later with half a dozen baskets full of goods.

"My God," Beth whispered.

We wouldn't need to go to a single other house now. This was everything we had set out for—if indeed the other nurses, who had been sent in different directions on a similar mission, fulfilled their parts as well.

"I hope this will be enough," our hostess said graciously, and I thought, *"Will it."*

Beth laughed. "We must say, we're very surprised. Nobody else has been willing to help us so far."

She laughed. "Oh, they're just simple folk. I know which side should prevail, and I'm sure you do, too."

As Beth and I each gathered a basket in our arms, our hostess smiled broadly.

"Best of luck to your boys," she said.

We returned to camp with an abundance.

We, of course, did not have to carry much. Our delicate backs could not bear the same load as the men carried in their packs, so our supplies were put in a large wagon that tottered along behind the men. We marched beside it.

From my vantage point, I could see Joshua, and I kept a careful eye on him the whole time. He was marching in step just as well as the rest of them, only falling out of pace a few times and then quickly correcting himself. For anyone not familiar, he could have been like any of the rest of them. He could have been a man.

"So I heard," Beth was telling me, "that some of the companies don't even give orders in English! Have you heard of the Zouaves? Oh, and there's one—Lord help me, I can't remember the name—but anyhow, all the orders are in German. Imagine that! The United States Army, and they're giving the orders in Ger—Cassie? Cassie, what's the matter?"

Ahead, Joshua was starting to stumble. He kept trying to touch his back as if there were something wrong there.

"His wounds," I thought.

He still had the welts from that whipping a few days ago. Now he was holding up the line, and for several minutes, men were tripping around him.

Soon, a lesser officer was at Joshua's side, pulling him out of line. They exchanged fierce words, and when the officer grabbed his arm, Joshua yanked away. He gestured to his back, and the officer shook his head before shoving my brother back into the line.

"What just happened?" Beth asked, evidently noticing what I was seeing.

"I don't know. The officer probably just scolded him for disturbing the march."

But Joshua had a terrified look on his face, and something didn't feel right.

When we arrived at camp, I discovered what they'd been

discussing.

The screams were piercing. If they were bad before, they were excruciating now, and the worst was that I could hear how he was trying to keep them in. It sounded excruciating.

"God's bones," I whispered, and when I set off to find him, Beth trailed along behind me, presumably to make sure I didn't do anything stupid.

If this was what I thought it was—and I knew it was—I was going to do something *really* stupid.

"Lord in Heaven," Beth whispered as we came upon the sight.

"*No*!" I screamed, and the dozen-strong crowd flicked their eyes toward me for a second. "No." A sob was coming on.

I plowed through the crowd and pushed past an officer, trying not to look at the sight ahead as I made my way toward it.

"Ma'am," the officer called, grabbing my arm. "I can't let you go any farther."

"That's my brother!" I hissed. "Let me go!"

"Ma'am."

"Oh, God. Look at him! Why are they doing this? Who allowed it?"

"It's Captain's orders, ma'am."

"Then to Hell with the captain."

The words curled on my tongue. I was so, so close to speaking them. I felt like I was going to crumble, that my knees would give way and I would become a heap of nothingness. Perhaps the earth would swallow me whole.

The officer had released my arm, and Beth now grabbed it.

"Cassie, there's nothing you can do."

"I can't believe this. I can't *believe* that captain. He will rot in Hell, he will."

"Cassie!" she gasped. "Do not speak such words."

"What? Would you say it isn't true? Look at him!"

The welts were gaping open now, red and raw. It looked worse than torture—just watching it, in fact, was torture.

"I will get revenge on this captain," I whispered, not even sure that Beth could hear me. "I will get revenge."

Joshua was released from the post, and he stumbled past the crowd, nearly weeping, toward the hospital tent.

If a heart could break in half, mine did then.

I followed him quickly, such that he could probably hear my footsteps behind him, but he did not turn to acknowledge me in his haste to arrive in the tent. The nurse's eyes popped open at the sight of him, and she ducked out of the way as he dove into the nearest bed. He was not weeping, but he looked like he wanted to, and I for one would not have blamed him for it.

"What in God's name happened to him?" the nurse, whom I recognized as Mary, asked.

"The whipping post," I replied, seething with rage. "They whipped over his old wounds."

Mary closed her eyes. "Oh, God." She pressed a hand to her forehead. "Those were infected."

Well. That explained why Joshua had been stumbling while he marched. The fact that he'd marched smoothly before then was a feat of remarkable strength. I retrieved a cloth and some ointment and started to dab over the open wounds. "Why was he cleared to march, then?"

"To march?"

"Yes. He was whipped for stumbling while he marched."

"What kind of captain would do such a thing, if the boy was obviously injured?"

My lip trembled. "A monster."

Joshua winced with pain.

"I'm sorry," I whispered.

Mary shook her head.

"Well, he wasn't cleared to march. You know how it works here. Nobody in their right mind would have sent him out like that."

I tried to recall the day before the march. After retrieving those baskets of food, I'd visited Joshua once before nightfall. His wounds had healed, but only slightly, and he hadn't talked much, but he'd put on a facade of strength and tried to insist that he was okay.

"Joshua," I asked, cringing as he winced again, "Who cleared you to march?"

I heard the word, but it was muffled because his face was pressed against the cot.

"Nobody."

"Nobody?"

"I went out myself."

I lifted my head toward Heaven and closed my eyes.

"You decided to disobey the nurses' orders," I breathed as I said, "and march with *infected wounds*?"

His head made a small movement that I assumed to be a nod.

"Joshua," I whispered. "You have to take care of yourself."

He groaned. I didn't ask him to explain; I already knew why he'd done it. Because he was foolish, and he thought he could do many things that he could not, in fact, really do. "Joshua," I sighed, with the intention to say something else.

I worked at his wounds for hours, too horrified to even scold him as I would normally be inclined to do. Perhaps an hour before sunset, another nurse tapped my shoulder.

"I'm taking a shift. Would you like me to— " she gestured at my brother, who had fallen asleep.

My instinct was to say no, to stay with Joshua until every lash had scabbed over, but I had someone to see.

Once out of the tent, I found Georgeanna in a matter of minutes. She was sitting by the fire in the hospital camp, tapping her knee along to a distant violin melody back at the soldiers' camp. Upon seeing me, she immediately stood. Her eyes were sympathetic, and she appeared to be scanning me as if trying to decipher how I was feeling. She knew about the whipping—everybody did—although not in detail, and she no doubt wondered whether I would be spitting rage or whether I was a pinch away from heavy weeping. And the funny thing was, I was both, but one much more than the other.

Down by the creek, where we ended up sitting, I watched the fish swimming under the clear water while Georgeanna waited for me to speak.

"Henry," I eventually said quietly, "do you have a pistol?"

He nodded.

I sniffed. "I'm going to need it."

"In God's name, what for?"

"I cannot tell you. I just need it. I'll give it right back. Will you trust me?"

"If you would tell me the reason, I might."

I gritted my teeth.

"God dammit!" I hissed, and Henry flinched in surprise at my curse. "Henry, you have to help me. I just need you to give me that pistol."

"If you tell me what you intend to do with it."

I couldn't say it aloud. It was stupid, irrational, and he would laugh at me, but I had this rage, this deep, deep rage that now permeated my every thought, and I knew it would not cease until I got revenge for my brother. If his condition worsened, if—God forbid it—he became gravely ill, I would make the captain pay. And I would need that pistol to do it.

"Never mind," I replied. "It was only a thought."

"I pray that you will voice it."

I sighed, absentmindedly drawing a small line in the dirt.

"If anything happens to my brother because of this," I asserted, "then in God's name, I will have my revenge on that captain."

He laughed, and it was the kind of laugh that said, *"How naive and foolish you are,"* the kind of laugh that was so frustrating and humiliating that, just for a second, I wanted to punch him.

"You want to shoot him?"

I didn't say anything. If I said, *"I might,"* he would have laughed that infuriating laugh again.

Henry sighed and placed his hands on his bent knees.

"I don't know why you would want to do such a thing just because your brother was sent to the post again."

"You don't understand. He was marching with infected wounds."

He sucked in a breath.

"They lashed him while he had the wounds?"

Nod.

"And the captain knew about this?"

Again, nod. And then a deep sigh.

"This is the way of things here."

"I'm worried about Joshua. If the infection gets worse —

God, I can't even bear to think of what can happen, but the captain must pay."

"Who sent Joshua out marching with those wounds?"

"Nobody. Joshua went out of his own doing."

Henry leaned his back against a tree.

"Well, then the captain can plausibly say that it was Joshua's fault. He decided to go out marching knowing the consequences."

"Don't try to blame this on him," I hissed. "Joshua is sixteen. He doesn't know what he's doing."

"He knows more than you give him credit for." Henry laughed softly but not humorously and took out a cigarette. "You must understand," he continued as he lit, "I'm just trying to explain to you how the army works. If Captain Bradford does something, it's to keep order. I'm sorry about your brother, all right? But you can't do something drastic just because you're upset."

"What the captain did was cruel, and you know it."

"I do," he replied calmly. "But this is a cruel place."

I sat up straighter, and as Henry puffed a cloud of smoke in the other direction, I folded my arms. I didn't want to even think it, but I had to say it.

"If Joshua dies, or is otherwise seriously injured, will you give me that pistol?"

Henry shook his head.

"I can't."

"Fine."

I stood and brushed off my skirt. I would have to find somebody else to help me. It would be difficult, but with the captain being so evil, *somebody* else must be angry enough with him to help me get what I needed.

After exactly three steps away, Henry spoke.

"Wait."

He was puffing out another cigarette, an image of leisure against that tree with one leg bent and the other stretched out.

"Don't go too far. There might be another way."

"Really?"

A sigh.

"Well," he began.

Chapter Six

After marching for three days more, we made camp. We were in Tennessee now, apparently, and the word was that the enemy was close. "We won't be fighting until more men arrive." This was the story told around the fire. "We don't know how many the Rebels have." As it was, our numbers were immense—there must have been tens of thousands. There was hardly enough room for everybody because most of the land was overgrown, but we all squeezed into patches of the field.

Next day, gunshots. It wasn't the scale of a full battle, but it sent a shiver down my spine. At first, they could have been mistaken for a dropped pot, but then it became clear what they were. Henry tried to ease my worry by telling me it was just a skirmish, but I was not used to this. I did not know what it meant to have the enemy so close.

The captain gathered our company for orders. As a nurse, I technically wasn't supposed to listen, and the truth was that hardly any of the few hundreds of us could hear, but what he said was this: "There have been many skirmishes these past hours, and under the orders of General Grant, I am told to remind you not to provoke battle with our enemy. We are not to enter battle until the General commands. Is that clear?"

"Aye, sir," echoed the men.

I was trying not to express the rage that bubbled at the very sight of the captain. Hands around his throat, a knife in his side—oh, I was imagining the possibilities. Or better yet, that pistol. But there was, perhaps, the other way.

After the orders, the men dispersed, and Henry was again by my side.

"No duties today?"

He grinned. "I don't know if you've seen the men, but it's unbuttoned collars and cards in the grass today."

I had seen them. It was the picture of laziness.

"Cards?

Hasn't the captain banned it?"

"Ah, they don't let him see. He's been away taking orders, or he hides away in his tent. Lord only knows what he's doing in there for so long."

"Bastard," I thought. *"He's a bastard."*

There was truly no reason to think it—as if taking orders or staying in one's tent was a crime—but I could not think of him without mentally uttering such a phrase.

"Have you any news about—" I looked around. No, it wasn't wise to speak freely of such a thing. "About what we spoke of?"

Henry nodded. "See that fellow there, with the dark hair? He rightly volunteered. And to think I was afraid to speak of it. Well, I did not speak of it directly at first, but when it came up in the discussion, well," he shrugged as he said, "it was very lucky."

"Lucky indeed," I murmured, still staring at the dark-haired man. I touched his arm.

"Henry," I said meaningfully, "I cannot thank you enough for this."

He shrugged, but he looked worried. For me? Surely not. Perhaps for himself, then.

"There's a lot I would do for you."

I wasn't sure how to interpret that.

I could feel the world ending. Or at least it seemed that way, with the booming cannons, the scattered cries, and the more abstract but no less distinct terror. In the masses was the dark-haired man of a few days past, the one whom Henry had pointed out to me. Should this man succeed, these terrible things would all be worth it.

I shivered. I could not believe I had gone this far.

Georgeanna appeared at my side.

"They'll be coming in soon, surely. It's a wonder we've hardly any yet."

There were five patients now, all currently being cared for, which left most of us nurses to stand idle. I was tempted to sneak a swig of the spare whiskey, just to distract myself, or to feel the burn, or both. It would help me through today, at the very least. But I knew better.

"May we pray that this day is not so bloody," she concluded.

"A little blood, rightly spilled, can be a good thing," I replied cryptically.

For a moment she appeared shocked, and I wondered if she suspected me. But I had committed no real crime. I had put a bullet through no man's head. I was, at best, just stirring fire.

"I would disagree," she replied, distant.

I was not sorry to see her leave my side. A little time alone would be a benefit: I could say a prayer for my brother and for the men. And, perhaps, one for myself.

I moved out of the relative seclusion of the ring of hospital tents to better see the carnage. I had never seen so much red in my life. It was hard to focus on a single thing; here, a horse was screaming as a blade meant for its master slashed its side hard enough to expose bone, and there, a soldier clutched a horribly bleeding eye that appeared to have been bullet-struck. Why Joshua had chosen this I doubted I would ever fully comprehend. But I understood a little better now.

"Cassie!" I heard. "Cassie!"

I turned, and a nurse named Lise was calling my name.

"Come help."

Hardly two minutes later, I found myself pressing the heel of my palm into a young man's chest. My hands were wet with his blood.

"Ah—ah," he gasped, eyes closing, and I started to feel it: the lives slipping away like wet mud.

I was useless as a nurse.

The patient died under my hands, and I didn't even have time to wipe the blood. What a sight for the next sorry fellow.

He came in, tall and lanky and young, curled brown hair, eyes blue and bright. His face was mostly obscured by dirt, but I knew him; I would know him anywhere. I felt my whole body change in an instant. My insides felt thin, as if they would start to simply pour out of me like sand.

"No," I whispered. "No."

In my wicked distraction, I had forgotten. I had forgotten what could happen to my brother. The devil must have been laughing then, for there it was: the moment I let my worry slip away, it all came true.

"No!" I cried. "Joshua!"

I made quite a ruckus as he was lowered from the stretcher onto one of the shallow cots. His eyes were closed, and the hole was in his leg. Lise was by his side, unwrapping a bandage, but I pushed her—a little too rudely—out of the way.

"Let me do it," I gasped. "I'll do it."

She huffed and stepped back.

And so it began. With my bloody hands, I bandaged his leg as tightly as I could and prayed that it would stop the bleeding.

"Joshua," I whispered when done, holding his dirt-stained face, "Joshua, answer me." He appeared to have passed out. I slapped his cheek. "Joshua!"

He couldn't have lost enough blood to pass out, could he? My bandage had stopped the bleeding.

His eyes were closed, his lips drooping.

"Dear Lord," I prayed, *"let him wake. Lord, let him wake."*

It all started to come back. Him playing horses with me, jumping on my back and making me crawl on all fours—I often ended up with scraped and splintered knees from our house's rough wooden floor. Him trying to sing "John Brown's Body" but getting half the words wrong. Wrestling with him and pretending to lose until the days I didn't have to pretend anymore. Hearing him say, "*I love you, Cassie*" and knowing he meant every word. Hugging him so tight that his breath caught and he started giggling uncontrollably. Holding onto him and letting him hold onto me on the days we didn't recognize our own mother and on the days she didn't seem to recognize us.

"Joshua," I whispered, "you have to come back to me."

His breath, ever so faint, picked up.

I wrapped my hand in his in order to feel his faint pulse but also just to hold him because lately, I'd forgotten what it was like to be so close to him. I'd forgotten what it was like to hear him say, *"Cassie"* the way some boys said, *"Mama."* I'd forgotten what it was like to squeeze his hand in hard times, to whisper, *"God is watching over us,"* and to hear him whisper it back like I was the one in need of comfort. So I squeezed his hand now, whispered, "God is watching over us," and pretended that he was squeezing back because this time I really did need comfort.

"Cassie, I need help over here," Lise called in a thin voice over the incessant shrieking and praying of the patients.

I turned to her with tears in my eyes, and she sighed as if I had offended her somehow.

"Never mind."

His pulse was waning. My throat tightened in panic. I usually didn't call for the doctor when it was this busy, but what choice did I have? I couldn't let this happen. I couldn't let Joshua—

"Doctor Gardner! Doctor Gardner!" I cried, but I knew he was nowhere near. "Lise, get the doctor!"

"I'm a little busy at the moment, Cassie!" she replied thinly.

Thump. Pause. Pause. Pause.

Oh, no. No, no, no. *No.*

"Joshua!"

Thump.

There it was again, but I could feel him slipping from my fingers. He was not a young man of sixteen any longer, but a small child. A boy who would cling to my leg and force me to walk with him weighing down my ankle. The boy who linked his arms with mine to spin in circles until we fell, laughing uproariously. The boy who would whisper, "*I love you, Cassie*" like it was a great secret but also the most obvious thing in the world.

He squeezed my hand ever so slightly, and it was as if he was saying it one last time: "*I love you, Cassie*."

I bent my head over his body and wept. I clutched at his shirt, at his bloody trousers. I pressed my hands to his cheeks and tried to shake him back awake. This couldn't be happening; God's will was in my favor. I had known so deeply, so surely, that everything would somehow be okay. How could this, then, happen?

Some time later—maybe it was fifteen minutes, maybe an hour—Lise pulled my shoulder.

"Cassie, I need your help."

I could not help. How could I help, when the world had ended? How could I go on? How could *anyone* go on?

"No," I whispered.

I felt empty inside. There was a deep, deep hole that would never be filled.

But the men needed to be cared for, and who would do it if not me?

I was three seconds away from forcing myself from Joshua's bedside to help when Lise huffed and said, "Fine, if that is your will," and left me to my weeping.

Hours later, they brought him in. He was groaning and clutching his side. Lise looked at me darkly.

"I'll take him."

"No," I said. "He's mine."

I dressed the captain's wounds as usual, tearing the bandage and tying it up.

He grunted. "Damn Rebels."

I smiled. "It's not always the Rebels, Captain, who do you harm."

Rage pulsed through me, shocking and unfamiliar, and laced my words. It was not the captain's fault, I knew—it had not been his bullet, after all—but it had been his whips, indeed, that scarred my brother. For his cruelty, to Joshua and others, he had to pay. And he was paying now, wasn't he—ever so dearly.

So I bandaged his wounds, as was my job—and I did it well, too—but secretly, I hoped the bandage would not work. Secretly, I hoped that his heart would stop.

"Forgive him," Henry would say. *"You can't let this get out of control. You have to forgive him."*

The captain grunted, "What do you mean?"

I glanced at Joshua, at his body.

"What, is that your brother? The one who was stupid enough to march with an injury?"

"You could have killed him."

He shrugged and glanced at Joshua.

"Wouldn't matter now, would it?"

With trembling hands, I placed a flask of whiskey in his hand.

"Drink up, Captain," I advised. "You'll feel better."

Twenty minutes later, when I glanced over from the cot-side of another soldier, he hadn't even touched the whiskey.

As the battle came to a close, Beth, who had all day been working in another tent, found me standing mournfully over Joshua. I must have had an expression of utter hopelessness because she knew something was wrong. She knew something was crushingly, irreparably wrong.

"Cassie," she said, coming beside me and wrapping her arm around my side, "Who is this?"

What was she talking about? Was she blind?

"Joshua."

Was it not obvious?

She looked disbelieving.

"Are you sure? I can hardly see his face for all the dirt."

"It's Joshua," I said. "Look, he even has the—" I reached for the necklace, the one I'd given him before Bull Run.

It wasn't there. The Joshua I knew would never have removed it from his neck. But did I really know him anymore?

Of course, I did. There had to be some other explanation.

"Cassie," Beth said reassuringly, and it was infuriating. "I don't think it's him."

"Of course, it's him! I've been watching over him for hours now. Do you honestly think I wouldn't know?"

Beth huffed. "Fine. You don't have to believe me. But you're mourning for a brother who isn't yours."

With a puff of air, she was gone.

God, what was wrong with her? Of course, it was Joshua. This was his unruly hair, his bright creamy eyes, his long spindly limbs, the birthmark on his neck—

I squinted. The birthmark wasn't there. Perhaps I was looking in the wrong place? But no, it was easy to see. No necklace, no birthmark—

God's bones.

The boy did look eerily similar. And with the face so dirty, he was easily mistaken for my brother. But how could I not have noticed? I had wrapped these wounds, I had whispered reassurances, and I had wept. I had wept over this body, and I had felt my heart spill out onto this musty cot; I had lost everything. And this boy wasn't even Joshua.

Oddly, I didn't feel any better now than before. The deep emptiness in my stomach didn't go away. How could this have happened? I would have known my brother anywhere. I would have known him *anywhere*.

"It's all right, Cassie," Beth whispered when I found her outside an hour later. "You're just so stressed lately—it was a trick of the mind. It happens."

I appreciated her sympathy, but her voice was unsure, and I was left with an unsettling truth: this *didn't* happen. If I couldn't recognize my own brother, something was terribly wrong.

Beth and I continued on our afternoon walk. I was still fragile, and in my shock, I seemed not to have fully realized that my brother was still alive, that I hadn't truly lost him. The incredible grief that had hardened in my chest was not gone, and I was left with an unshakable misery.

"I'm sorry," I told Beth, who had a hand on my shoulder as we approached the camp. "It's terrible. He's not dead, not like I thought he was, and I still…" I sniffled.

"It's all right, Cassie," she replied sincerely. "Even though you didn't lose him, it's still something awful."

She did understand, I was certain. Even though Beth and I didn't know each other well—I didn't know her birthplace, for God's sake, or how many siblings she had, or anything of that sort—we knew the most important things about each other. I had seen her in probably her worst moment, and she was seeing me in mine, and even though I didn't know her last name or her religion, it didn't matter. I knew everything I needed to.

We passed the soldiers' camp. The men were gambling, as usual, and it was surreal how cheerful they were. If not for the bloodstained uniforms and the dirt smudged on their faces, an onlooker would never have guessed how they had toiled today.

"How do they do it?" I wondered.

I was still grieving over a boy I didn't know, and they had stumbled through Hell on earth, and they seemed to brush it right off.

"There's Joshua," Beth pointed out, and I was gripped with uncertainty at the sight of him. I could not tell him of my episode today, but I would not sleep right until I had some physical reassurance that he was still here: a shake of the hand or a hug. I doubted he would consent to either.

"Just go talk to him," Beth urged. "You'll feel better."

I hadn't a clue what she knew of it, but I nervously obliged. I felt like a child. Still, I made room next to my brother on the coarse dirt and listened to the nearby fiddler.

"Joshua."

He turned.

"Cassie. How are you?"

I gulped and lied. "Great. I'm great."

"Good."

He inclined himself awkwardly toward the fiddler again.

"Joshua," I echoed. "I'm glad you made it back all right today."

"Thanks, Cassie." He pressed a hand to my shoulder for just a second before letting it fall away. "I'm glad, too."

After that, I was nearly okay. Almost, but not quite. Because while we sang and laughed together that night, I knew that something was wrong. Here was my brother, the most precious person in the world to me, and somehow he was a stranger now.

"*I would recognize Joshua anywhere,*" I had thought so surely. And yet I had not.

Chapter Seven

Next morning, before daylight, I confronted my brother. I could not get that image out of my head—well, there were many images I could not remove from my memory— but imagining him without that necklace under his uniform made me shudder.

Before the men prepared to go out, I found my brother.

"Joshua!" I called, embracing him briefly and, as we pulled apart, put a hand on his shoulder. "Be careful, understand?"

He smiled and hoisted his rifle over his shoulder.

"Of course. I will be just fine."

He said it so surely, and I almost believed him.

The gunfire started just after the sun rose, and most of us were now numb to the pain. Or at least, I assumed. I caught one of the nurses shuddering from a particularly loud crescendo of firing but nothing more. Beth was in a tent with me this time. I was glad for her company, although we had little time to talk besides an occasional "Will you pass the bandages there?" and a solemn nod whenever we caught each other's eye. The captain seemed to be recovering, unfortunately. He had been relocated to a hospital in the camp instead of near the battle lines, but I knew of his state because a group of soldiers had been gossiping mercilessly about it the night before. I hoped he rotted in that tent.

I was in the process of moving a corpse—that of a blond-haired man I might have had my eye on had I the chance—off its cot when a small slip of paper fell from the coat pocket. I picked it up and quickly pocketed it.

However, in the process of lowering the body—a task usually assigned to two of us or to a few of the men, but there weren't enough nurses for that at the moment—I felt a small movement. Was he really dead? God's bones, I had just assumed it because he had been still so long. I checked the pulse. Faint, but definitely still there.

Ugh. Back on the cot, then. What a fool was I—usually if their eyes were closed and they weren't moving, there was only one reason for it, but I should have checked anyhow.

At the end of the day, when Beth and I were stepping out for a small break—with all the wounded, we would likely be working until we dropped dead, and if not for the darkness that made it near-impossible to work—God knew we didn't have enough oil lamps to make much of a difference—we would probably have labored through the night. As it was, we would be doing whatever we could despite the lack of light. However, at nightfall, Beth and I both deemed it time to finally eat something, and as we stepped outside the tent, we grabbed the bits of hardtack we'd brought with us.

Neither of us said a word about the work we'd done that day. It was impossible to speak of it. So we munched quietly into the still night, aware that in the blackness was a ground covered in bodies and blood; it was the devil's field now.

I was absentmindedly fishing around in my pockets when I found the small paper.

"Oh," I said, retrieving it. "Look here—I must have picked this up earlier." Beth couldn't see it, of course. "It's a paper. Must be a letter."

Beth hummed. "Let's read it! Maybe it's a love letter."

"Oh, come. It might be very private. It's none of our business."

"Oh, it'll be fine. Besides, they're all the same, anyway. 'Timmy, I miss you ever so dearly. I am praying that God will bring us back together again soon.'"

"We can't read it without any light."

"Wait a moment. I'll go inside and grab a candle."

"Beth, you—"

But it was too late.

She emerged seconds later with the object. This all seemed like a lot of trouble for a meaningless letter, but we both needed a break from what we'd done that day, and to Beth, at least, there was nothing better suited to defuse stress than the private information of other people. Of course, she would be deeply offended if someone had so delved into *her* letters, but apparently, this was not a consideration. She pored over the contents for a few minutes, and I nudged her to read it aloud, but she shushed me. Whatever; I would read it after, however poor my reading skills were.

"Cassie," she whispered in awe. "Dear God. Look at this!"

I glanced over the letter. "Lines…troops…Sunday…"

"Did you get this from an officer?" she asked. "It must have been an officer."

"He looked like a private to me. He had the one row of buttons on his coat."

"These are a commanding officer's papers, Cassie. They might even be General Grant's. Why would a private have them?"

"Maybe he was delivering a message."

Beth snorted. A messenger would not have ridden through the front lines of battle; it was highly unlikely that one would be steered into the hospital with a bullet in his leg. So why did the man have these papers?

"There's only one explanation, Cassie."

Beth blew out the candle, which was dripping precariously close to its saucer and made her next words sound eerie.

"Whoever had this is a spy."

I considered the handsome young man, who I'd thought to be dead.

"Are you sure? Maybe he just picked it up somewhere. The officers aren't careful with their papers, you know. By God, he might not even have known what they were."

"Cassie, almost everyone can read. Even if he couldn't, why would he have kept this paper? It obviously wasn't a letter from someone's mother, and even if it was, he wouldn't have had a reason to keep it. No, it was nearly unmistakable, even to the illiterate. The seal at the bottom of the page designated it as an officer's letter and no other."

"I don't know. Why did *I* take it from him? It was a thoughtless thing."

"No, Cassie, you had reason to do it."

She touched my arm.

"But you can't be caught with that paper."

"Well, what am I to do? Slip it back into his coat? What if somebody sees me?"

"You have to report it."

I sighed.

"Beth, this could all be nothing. I'm sure it's not even an important paper, after all. The officers send plenty of communications such as…well, I don't know, but they can't all be very important."

"You can't risk it, Cassie. We have to turn it in."

"To whom? The captain?"

"To whoever is in charge while the captain is infirm. I'll find the colonel tomorrow and tell him what you found. All you have to do is give him the papers and say whom you got them from."

She stood, brushing off her dress, and started to walk away.

"Where are you going? I thought we weren't done talking."

The wind shuddered through the nearby trees, giving us both chills.

"Well, there's not much else to talk about, is there? You'll do the right thing or you won't."

I knew. I knew that I should turn those papers in. But what would happen to the man with these papers? What if we had misunderstood, and the situation was not as we thought it was? I knew the captain was not the kindest of men.

There was another thought, though, that came to me in Joshua's voice.

"*It is our duty to stomp out all forms of treachery. There is nothing more important than our Union."*

That, I was certain, was what he would have told me.

"Okay," I said. "Fine."

The lieutenant sniffed and focused on the paper, and then his eyes grew wide.

I was still not sure about this.

"God's blood." He glanced at me. "Who had this?"

"I don't know his name, sir, but he's in the hospital. I can point him out."

"Get his name. And report back to the colonel. I'll send a lieutenant with you. We may very well have a spy on our hands."

"I do hope it is not so."

An hour later, I was slipping through the flaps of the colonel's tent with the name rattling around in my head: *Alexander Farnese.* Was it truly the name of a criminal? He had seemed soft-spoken and kind when I asked him for the information.

"Private in the Pennsylvania 25th," he'd even offered, voice weak.

"He might not even survive to be tried," I thought. *"Is it really worth it?"*

I could have given the paper to Beth: "You take it, and decide what must be done."

But I would not shy from responsibility. I had a duty to the commanding officers, and they would exact justice as they saw fit—*only* as they saw fit.

As long as that damned captain stayed in the infirmary, at least.

The colonel thanked me quickly for the information, and I hesitated before I exited the tent.

"Yes, madam?" he asked.

"I just hope that I have not incriminated someone who is

innocent," I said, unsure whether it was even appropriate to say it.

"Whether he is guilty or innocent, we will find the truth," the colonel assured. "You can trust us."

A gust of wind assaulted me as I stepped outside.

Henry stepped into the tent as the birds chirped good-morn. The battle had been well-won yesterday, and the men had celebrated with every sort of debauchery. I would have expressed surprise that the captain even allowed it, but he wasn't really in a state to be enforcing rules—at least not as strictly as he had done before.

"Cassie."

I was a little busy at the moment—the hospital was still full, and amputations would likely run into the next few days. Thus, we wouldn't march for about a week. That was the hope, at least.

"How do you do, Henry," I replied, making a real effort to be polite, even though I was too busy to actually look his way.

"I'm faring well. Captain's recovered."

I tore a bit of bandage with my teeth.

"Really."

The lad I was dressing was half-asleep, by my observation; he was hardly eavesdropping. As for Alexander Farnese, possible spy, I hadn't heard a word of his fate. I preferred not to think about it, but it itched in the back of my mind like a nasty bite.

"He almost died, Cassie."

"Shame."

I tied the bandage, then moved on to the next patient. Henry followed.

"Cassie, what happened was a mistake. Timothy's been having nightmares every night about it."

"Is that what you came here to tell me, that your friend is having nightmares? Well, I'm sorry for it."

"Agh. No, Cassie, it's not just that. Don't you understand? This was a mistake."

"I'm sorry if you think so, but it's too late now, so I don't know why you're telling me this."

He stepped farther into my vision.

"You can't just do things like this. *We* can't do things like this. There must be something wrong with you if you don't regret this even a little bit."

Finished with my current patient, I rose from his bedside and stepped around Henry.

"Now isn't a good time for this discussion."

"Can we talk about it later, then? I'll come find you when you're on break."

"Sure, Henry."

I was close to saying it outright: *"No. There's nothing to speak about."*

He had regrets, I did not. There was little more to it.

"Cassie." He touched my arm. "Don't be short with me. Please, in God's name, hear me."

It was good that he gave up and left before I could respond because I didn't have anything to say.

I didn't speak to Henry. It would be plausible to say that I didn't get a chance, but the truth was that I didn't want to. Everything lately was so overwhelming, and I didn't want to be roped into regretting what I had done. The other thing was, why was Henry doing this? Did he not understand how stressed I felt? Did he think his worries about me were of paramount importance? Maybe he was just being thoughtful, but it was of no use to me.

Still, when the spy stood in front of the firing squad, Henry stood beside me.

My stomach dropped as the officers made him stand on the box. I wondered if they would read the charges. Everyone in the camp knew about it, though. Some of them had vehemently insisted that he couldn't have done it. I hadn't heard Henry's word about it. I wasn't sure whether I cared to hear it, now.

"You heard what happened, didn't you?" he whispered in my ear.

I nodded.

"I did hear. How awful."

I caught Beth's eye; she was standing arm-in-arm with Nicholas, and when she stared solemnly back at me, I knew what she was thinking: *"It was the right thing to do. You may not like it, but it was."*

I turned away.

"Do you think he's guilty?" I asked Henry.

"I didn't know him, personally. But a friend of mine will swear on his grave that Farnese would never do it. Personally, I think it just shows how sometimes you don't know someone as well as you think you do."

"Oh, really," I said trivially, but his words had sounded accusatory.

I tried to ignore it.

Well, there was nothing else to it. He'd been found with the papers, and according to a rumor, they had found that all his brothers were fighting for the Rebels in Virginia. The makings of a spy if there ever was one.

But there was no way to be sure. They cocked their rifles, and at the very last second before they took their shots, he looked me straight in the eye. Not angry, not betrayed, just sad.

Then they did it.

I had only passed out for a second, apparently—one of the nearby nurses had pulled out a vial of smelling salt to revive me, bless her—but when I woke up, I found myself in Henry's arms.

Deliberately not facing the scene behind us, I stood up and took a few deep breaths.

"Are you all right?" Henry asked.

I nodded, still lightheaded.

"I'm just—not accustomed to such things."

He didn't know what I had done. Hopefully, he never would.

As far as I was concerned, it was just another battle. The men had skirmished themselves back to Virginia, and we had followed with bandages in one hand and bottles of chloroform in the other. Beth was many months pregnant now, but her swollen figure was well-hidden by her dress and truly, she had not gained much weight at all. Sometimes I asked her whether she was really still fit to work, but she would only reply, "I've got a job to do," and that would be the end of the conversation. I wondered if she would work until the second she had to push the child out of her. I had no idea what she was going to do. Nobody knew about it except me, and it seemed that she wasn't going to tell—she would be relieved of her nursing duties, certainly. There were a number of families who followed the soldiers at a fair distance, and there were enough infants and young children among them that Beth and her child would fit right in with that crowd. I didn't see anything terribly wrong with that, but I wondered if she feared it.

Alas, on a day of battle, the time came. When the trumpets sounded for the morning, Beth—on a bedroll beside me—groaned.

"No," she said. "I cannot."

"Is it time?" I asked.

Beth groaned.

"It's today," she replied. "It will be today."

"I shall get Nicholas."

She reached out with her arm. "No, don't. Today will be hard enough for him without this. He'll find out when he comes back."

I was prepared to argue, but I knew it was better to let it be. No captain would let him skip his duty, not to check on a pregnancy that by all camp rules was forbidden. Nicholas had slipped by in secret whenever he could, and if the next time he and Beth met under the cover of thick oaks, and she was carrying a child in her arms, then that would be the way of it.

So I sat with her while the others ate. She insisted that I eat something, too, so I took a bit of hardtack and sat with her, offering her small bites. Then the shooting started.

"You should go," she said. "They'll need you in the hospital."

"I can wait a little longer. They won't need me right away." What I meant was, *"I don't know how I'm going to leave you here."*

After an hour, she asked again, "Shouldn't you go?"

"I can't leave you, Beth."

"Oh," she sighed. "I wish I weren't keeping you from your duty."

I clasped her hand.

"I need to make sure that you're taken care of."

Maybe the physician would hold me in contempt when I came back, but no matter; I had no choice but to help Beth.

Eyes closed, she smiled. "Thank you."

It dawned on me then that if she delivered this baby today, I would not know how to help her. I had never done it before. I could appeal to one of the hospital nurses, but if I walked into that hospital, they would know we had shirked our duty, and even worse, they would know why.

The other option was to take her into town. The thought of disappearing from the camp was uncomfortable, but there would be ladies in town who could help, and there would be a bed there for Beth to lie down. Whether they would be willing to help was another story, but we would have to have faith.

It took some convincing—she didn't want to leave Nicholas—but finally, Beth agreed. She could hardly stand up, much less walk, but every horse was in battle now, so we were left without. Instead, she leaned on my shoulder and clutched her stomach as we slowly hobbled toward the nearest town.

By my estimation, it was only half a mile. Before we left, I had no idea how we would be able to walk farther than a few hundred feet, and as we walked, I had no idea how we were still doing it, but we trod on simply because we had no other choice.

The first house we came upon was empty, and Beth was sweating from exhaustion—I could feel the dampness on my shoulder—when we reached it. The next was half a mile farther, and I could feel my companion's resolve melting away. When we reached this next one, I knew, it would be the last of our walking, no matter if there was anyone in it or if they would let us enter.

I rapped weakly on the door.

After a long enough pause that made me suspect that the place was vacant, there was a stir from inside. A few excruciating seconds later, the door creaked open

"In God's name," came the voice, thickly accented. Then the woman noticed Beth, who was sweating and clutching her swollen stomach, and she softened. "What is this?"

"This woman is about to give birth, ma'am. At the moment, she has nobody and nowhere."

The woman, who was wearing a ragged gown that did little to diminish her aura of elegance, narrowed her eyes.

"Are you Yankees?"

On my shoulder, I felt Beth tense.

"Yes, ma'am," I said.

She crossed her arms.

"And why can't you help her?"

"I know nothing, ma'am. I've never assisted a birth before. And there's hardly a place for her to lie down back at camp. We haven't any supplies for this sort of thing."

She snorted. "But you think I can do something? In God's name, I can hardly find food. If I want to write letters, I have to make ink out of berry juice. I have nothing, thanks to the Yankees."

"Please, ma'am. She hasn't much time."

She let out a tired sigh and opened the door wider.

"There's a bed upstairs, but it might be easier to lay her on the sofa." She gestured straight ahead at the sitting room. "I'm going to look for some cloth."

Together, Beth and I hobbled to the room ahead.

"Cassie," she whispered, voice faint, "thank you."

"I would do it a thousand times more," I said sincerely.

The woman came back with a small armful of cloth and properly introduced herself. She was Laura, and she took our names graciously.

"You're very lucky, Beth," she said, presenting a small vial. "I found this."

Beth squinted. "What is it?"

"Just something to make the birth a little easier. But I won't give it to you yet."

From there we had nothing to do but wait. And we didn't have to wait long.

Before she started to whimper in pain, Beth said, "Cassie, if anything happens, he's yours."

I didn't know what she meant at first, but that was when she started gasping.

"It's time," Laura said.

She grabbed the bottle from the small table nearby and used it to wet a small cloth.

"Now, Beth," she continued, "you have to tell me you're okay with this. It's like a smelling salt but much stronger. When you wake up, it will be over and the whole thing will have been painless."

She hesitated on the world *when*. It sounded like she wanted to say *if*.

"Are you sure about this?"

"I've had many fine grandsons from it and no harm for it. It makes everything simpler."

Beth cried out suddenly and gasped, "By God, do it! I cannot take this!"

She clasped my hand as Laura put the cloth over her mouth, and then her grip slackened.

"She'll be all right," Laura assured me. "I've done four births and had no troubles yet."

It was an odd birth. I'd never witnessed one, but from what I'd heard it seemed a sweaty, loud, and altogether stressful affair. However, Beth hardly moved—Laura had Beth's legs opened and was working there, but there was hardly a movement.

It was very eerie.

Finally, Laura gasped quietly and gestured to me. "Come see."

And there it was: the head.

It was a calm affair. It was not earth-shattering. One second I was watching that tiny head pop out, and the next I had her in my arms—her. A girl. I wrapped her in the cloth I'd been holding and wiped off the blood. She screamed like the devil, but after a time in my arms, she looked up at me curiously, and I was ever so sorry that her first sight was not of her own mother. Perhaps it was fitting, though—had I not been there to intervene that fated night, she might not be here.

As soon as Beth's eyelids started to flutter, I brought her daughter over and began to lower her into Beth's arms. When I let the baby rest there, Beth was fully awake—if a little groggy—and she did not say a single word, just breathed a single, contented sigh.

That was when I knew without a single inkling of a doubt that smashing that bottle so many months ago had been the right thing to do.

"What is her name?" I asked.

She smiled down at her daughter. "I don't know. I suppose I should talk to Nicholas." She blinked. "I wonder if he's back yet."

"I wouldn't go out tonight," Laura said. "It's too close to sundown."

Beth wouldn't be able to go back to the camp in her condition, and the baby wouldn't be welcome, either—I would have to go there to fetch Nicholas and bring him back. Laura was right; I'd never make it there before dark, much less back here with Nicholas. No, it was best to wait till morning.

Beth sighed. "You're right."

"Then there's nothing to do," Laura sighed, "but wait."

Chapter Eight

The next morning, I returned to camp. I was at least hoping to find Nicholas to tell him the news, but I discovered a ripe sadness and desolation in the camp that quite worried me.

Henry was poking at the cinders of a long-dead campfire, staring into its depths as if it held answers. He jumped when I called his name.

"Oh, Cassie," he said, wiping his shirt awkwardly and standing to face me with an expression as if I were distinctly breakable, as if I would burst into hysterics at any moment.

"I'm looking for Nicholas," I informed him, growing ever more nervous by the expression on his face. "Is everything all right?"

"You haven't heard?" He bit his lip. "Oh, God, I'm so sorry—"

"What has happened? Is everything okay?" My blood ran cold. "Where is Joshua?"

"The Rebels licked us yesterday, Cassie, they really did, and we lost many of our men. I'm sorry to say it, but I think your friend's husband is among them."

"No, no, that cannot be!" I grabbed his hands. "Tell me it's not true. How can I find him? How can I know if he is alive?"

"Cassie, I need you to listen to me for a second."

"You need to help me find him! I'm not going back to Beth until I know with every drop of certainty that he has really passed."

"Cassie, there's something else."

My heart thumped.

"What?"

Henry wrapped his hands around my arm as if mapping it out.

"I don't know how to say this. I just don't know."

He dropped his hands and folded them across his chest.

"Your brother has been taken captive."

The whole world screeched to a halt.

“What?” I croaked.

“I’m so sorry, Cassie. I should have saved him. I should have been by his side—”

I did not know how sincerely he meant these words. It was not a soldier’s choice where he fell in the lines. If he was far from Joshua, it was not his fault. Still.

“Where are they taking him?”

“Last I heard, the soldiers were looking to settle in the town. But it’s only a rumor, Cassie. Don’t expect anything of it.”

“I have to go back,” I said, my voice hollow and unfamiliar.

Taken captive—what did it even mean? Would they trade him for some rotten Rebel prisoner, a man for a man? Or would they keep him locked up somewhere? No matter what, I knew this was not good.

Yet, Beth was depending on me now. I could not return without her husband or at least news of him. Could I?

“Are you certain, Henry, that you have no idea where Nicholas is?”

He shifted nervously.

“I’m sorry, Cassie. I wish I could help.”

“You can.” I fidgeted absentmindedly with my sleeve, then stilled my hand to say, “Find him.”

The journey back to town was long, longer even than it had been with the heavily pregnant Beth limping by my side. Still, I conquered the dusty path through the thick-leaved trees, fraught with worry and rough with determination.

I was going to get my brother back safely if it was the last thing I did on this earth.

My heart was pounding as I reached the town center. There were signs of soldiers all over: hoofprints in the dirt and of course distant shouts of conflict. The sound gave me shivers.

A scream pierced the air.

“Shut your goddamn Yankee mouth!” someone shouted.

After that, there were no words, only the sounds of a struggle. I ducked behind a nearby shop building to watch. I wanted to see what was happening before I charged into the middle of it. A small group of citizens, several dozens in number, had come to witness a cluster of soldiers who had gathered by a small fountain in the city's center; with them were at least half a dozen captives, or at least they must have been captives because of the ropes around their wrists and their nervous, harried expressions. I was too far to see any faces, but I was nearly certain that Joshua was not among them. They probably had at least a dozen captives, more than were here in my sight. He was somewhere else, certainly. I just had to find him.

I took a deep breath. What was I going to do? I couldn't charge into the Rebel camp and take my brother back; I'd never be able to overpower the soldiers. And our men weren't going to do anything about it, at least not for my sake only. If the captain had plans to get the captives back, maybe he would, but if he didn't, I could do nothing about it. Could I?

"God above," I prayed. *"What should I do?"*

"Here's the other one!" someone shouted gruffly.

I turned my attention back to the scene, still peeking from behind the building. He pushed a knobby-kneed, lanky boy to his knees and put a gun to his head.

This time, I had no doubt whatsoever whether it was my brother.

"No," I breathed and began to pant the word in a sort of crazed chant. *No, no, no.*

"What do you say, boys? I'm in the mood to shoot another goddamn Yankee."

The Rebels guffawed. "Shame that you're taking the opportunity from us, John. We have to keep some of them."

"Who said that?" He laughed.

The citizens jeered.

"Take another Yankee down!" "Shoot the tyrant!"

They were talking about the boy whose first word had been my name.

The gun was still pointed at Joshua's head. My whole life was contained in it, connected by an invisible thread to that wretched trigger.

The cheers grew louder. Without thought, except for blinding fear and an acute awareness of the hammering of my heart, I charged into the crowd, past the throng of now-shocked citizens, toward the spot where my brother was being held.

"No!" I cried. "Let him go! He's my brother, let him go!"

Joshua jerked his head to look at me.

"Cassie," he croaked, fear blazing in his eyes.

It was right then, in that moment, that I discovered what it was like to feel the whole earth shatter.

His captor grinned slyly at me.

"This little rat is your brother, then? Well, you might want to turn your head for this."

I tried, I tried, I tried to throw myself into his path. I was ready to take his bullet if I had to. But I was a tiny, tiny second too late.

The shot rang across the square, hammering in my ears, piercing my heart.

"No!" I screamed, collapsing at my poor brother's feet. "No, this can't be happening. Come back to me, Joshua, stay with me. I'm right here, I'm right here. Stay with me!"

For a single excruciating moment, Joshua glanced up at me. Blood was pooling in his mouth, and his eyes were closing—I was watching life drain out of him like water poured from a wooden cup.

"Cassie," he said.

And then he was gone.

I held his limp body in my hands for what could have been forever, rocking back and forth, back and forth while I wept. I could not feel anything, and I could not think. I was not here right now. I had not seen this. I had not caused it.

Then, after so much silence, a laugh echoed.

"That's what he gets for being a Yankee. Be thankful I didn't make you go with him."

"I wish you had," I thought. *"I wish I was with him now."*

I glanced back at the crowd. If I had been in someone else's place and not mine, maybe I would have seen some sort of sympathy in their eyes. Maybe I would have been able to detect some regret, some horror, but when I looked back at the crowd who had let this happen, I saw only jeering faces and angry eyes. I saw only monsters.

Eventually, people started to clear away. The soldiers took their living captives from the scene, and I did not lift my head to see them, but the poor men must have been terrified out of their minds. The crowd dispersed as if life would just go on from here, as if the world could still spin. And I stayed for hours and hours with my brother.

Many things could have prevented this. I could have listened to my instincts and found somewhere else for us to go. I could have warned Joshua to be more careful and for God's sake, to hold his tongue. I could have stayed in camp that day, left Beth with someone else, and been able to see Joshua being taken captive in enough time to follow the Rebels and demand him back.

I didn't know if any of those things would have worked, really, but they were a throbbing hurricane in my head. This was not real. This was not happening.

Someone knelt beside me; I could not see the face without turning my head, but it looked like a woman's.

"I'm so sorry," she said with a shaky voice. "None of us wanted this."

"Leave me alone," I hissed.

I did not see her again.

I did try to drag him back. In a burst of grief, I decided to pick him up and trek the half-mile back to Laura's house and perhaps bury him there—after all, I could not leave him here; I couldn't leave him alone. So I scooped him up like a babe.

After only a few steps, I knew it was no use. He was too heavy; I wasn't strong enough for this. In the middle of the dusty road, I laid him down and knelt helplessly by his side. *God, help me, help me. What do I do?*

The sound of marching soldiers rattled in the distance—the goddamned Rebels, probably, stomping their boots along a distant road, moving forward as if they had not taken everything from me.

Beth must be waiting for me. She would want to know about Nicholas —Oh, God, I would have to tell her about Nicholas—and she would need my help with the baby. My mind was buzzing to go back, but I could not make myself move from this spot. If the whole world were burning and God called upon me alone to save it, I would not be able to move from this spot. Except when the first blush of night began to fall.

"Joshua," I said as if he could hear me. "I'm so sorry. I'm so, so sorry."

Wind whistled through the trees as some kind of response.

I had no shovel to dig with, so I found some sticks to draw up the soggy earth. After what must have been an hour of primitive and frustrating digging, I might as well have not done any work at all—I had barely made a dent in the ground. But at least there was a sizeable pile of dirt I could cover him with—would it help much, I didn't know, but I could not stand the thought of vultures swooping down on him before he could be given a proper Christian burial.

I had seen soldiers buried this way before: in shallow graves, the dirt barely covering the mounds of their bodies. At least my brother would have been buried like a soldier, the way he would have wanted, but like this? Oh, it was a curse. He was all alone here, all alone, and I had no choice but to leave him.

"Lord," I prayed, not knowing a real funeral prayer but hoping God would forgive me for it, "watch over my brother in Heaven as you did on Earth. Give him strength. Give him courage. Give him grace and all the things he had in life while he is with you in Heaven. And Lord, give me the grace to honor his name. Give me strength"—I pressed a hand to my cheek as tears welled up—"give me strength to live without him."

My head dropped to his cold, lifeless chest, and my hands stroked his colorless cheeks. And it was in that moment, while I was whispering a tearful *Amen,* that I felt it. It was like someone had shot fire through my veins.

The Rebels had to die. Every last one of them: the one who had killed Joshua, everyone who had been there, and everyone who took up arms alongside them. Joshua was worth a hundred men to me, and that was how many should perish because of what had been done to him. Deep in my chest there was a sting. Somehow, I knew I would avenge him. Somehow I would make this right.

"God, forgive me," I whispered and kissed my brother one final time before making the long trek back to Beth.

I came into the house silently, like a ghost. Beth and little Elizabeth were asleep on a blanket on the floor, and the baby curled into Beth's chest. They looked so peaceful there, so blissful—how could I ever tell them about Nicholas? It would destroy them.

Laura emerged in the kitchen doorway, frowning when she saw my expression but saying nothing.

"It took you quite some time to come back," she stated finally.

I opened my mouth to respond, but I couldn't make words come out.

"Do you need tea? It tastes quite awful, to be honest—it's so awfully expensive these days, I had to use some old home-made stuff that I almost threw out years ago…Well, the point is, there's tea if you'd like some."

I didn't really have the energy to respond, but I tried to move my head enough to pass for a nod. She nodded back, but it was unclear whether she had understood.

Laura drifted back into the kitchen, and I was left alone with the sleeping mother and daughter. It was quite peculiar that they were here on the floor: Laura, if she was any kind of hostess at all, would have offered her bed. But perhaps she had, and Beth had refused. She would do such a thing.

I didn't want to be here. I didn't want to stand in front of Beth, watching her sleep unaware of the tragedy that had befallen her. I didn't want to think about the tragedy that had befallen *me*, either. A deep, gnawing sense of exhaustion washed over me. It seemed that nothing in this world could make me happy again.

"Here's some tea," Laura said, appearing in the doorway.

Her voice was quiet and solemn, more so than before.

I took the cup. It really did taste awful, but I was thirsty enough to take a few sips before an insatiable dissatisfaction washed over me. I didn't want anything to drink, and I didn't want anything to eat. I didn't want anything at all. I wanted to be away from here.

"Is everything all right?" Laura asked me carefully. I could tell she already knew the answer.

"Nicholas…" I mumbled, shaking my head. That was all I could say.

A long silence.

"We do have to tell her, you know," Laura replied finally.

We both glanced at the peaceful pair.

"How can we?" I thought. *"What do we say?"*

I didn't even want to think about it. I didn't want to think about any of this.

"Okay," I said. I took another sip of the tea, curling my tongue around the stale, bitter taste, and I gave it back. "I'm going outside."

Laura nodded at me as I crept across the room and through the back door.

"Cassie," she said, and although I wasn't sure if she even knew my full name, the use of the nickname touched my heart. "This will pass."

I'd heard that so many times in my life. Through a barren winter, when our stomachs growled fiercely and we cried out for food, Pa would say, *"It will get better."* In school, when I was sweating over a series of math problems, the older girl next to me would say, *"You'll figure it out. It'll be okay."* And I learned to say these things to Joshua, too. *"You'll make it through this. We'll be okay."* And that had been a lie. Laura's words echoed in my head, *"This will pass. This will pass,"* but it was little comfort. I knew they meant nothing.

The next morning, when we told Beth, she cried the whole day. Morning till night she wept, and I wanted to weep with her, but I hadn't the energy. I wanted to crawl into a dark hole and never come back out; I wanted to disappear. I wanted God to take me, too.

For weeks, the only time I really felt anything was when I would feel a spark of rage, a pinprick in my chest. I could kill those Rebel bastards; I could take up arms and shoot every last one of them. I could make them suffer.

Even little Elizabeth failed to move me. She cried often for her mother, and Beth would come with a ready breast, but food was scarce and thus her milk was, too. Laura and I shoveled all our portions toward Beth (which I would happily have done anyway, having nothing of an appetite lately), which meant that we hardly ate anything, but it was still grossly insufficient. We were lucky if she had a large potato and a few carrots each day. Elizabeth's wails were piercing, heartbreaking, but I could feel no true sympathy, only a false veneer—a remnant of the anguish and concern that I knew I *should* feel. I helped care for her, washing her face and soiled clothes and rocking her to sleep whenever Beth was too tired (though that was rarely successful at first, because the baby always cried for her mother), and I knew it was a good thing that I was here because otherwise, I would probably still be on that dusty road, kneeling over Joshua's body, but I sometimes wished that I had never left there. I didn't feel right here.

I had told Laura and Beth, eventually, about Joshua. Once Beth had ceased her own grief just enough to notice mine, she grew concerned, and I finally uttered the words: *"Joshua is dead."* And that was probably the most I ever spoke for several weeks.

Sometimes, when night fell and Laura retired to bed, Beth and I would sit together in the darkness: Beth because Elizabeth had woken, and I because I hardly slept these days. A candle would be lit, and we would absorb the silence or the sound of Elizabeth suckling. Grief hung over us both like a howling ghost, but it was more comforting in those moments than any other: there, with Beth close by feeling exactly as I did, the world felt a little less lonely, and God felt a little less far away.

And then morning would come, and Beth would be captivated with her baby, giggling and cooing to her, bending over her on the floor and coaxing her to lift her hands or to roll over, tickling her feet. A solemnity still lurked in her demeanor, but I couldn't help thinking, *"We are different."* It was terrible to lose a husband, sure as anything, but she had grown up without knowing him. She had lived without him before. I had never, not for a day in my life that I could remember, lived without Joshua. Now, the world was foreign, and I was lost. Beth had her baby, and I had nothing. And so we were different.

Elizabeth was lying on the coarse blanket on the floor, and Beth was hovering over her and kissing her forehead, eliciting tiny giggles. I sat quietly at the edge of the blanket, out of place because I wasn't participating but with nowhere else to go.

Laura appeared at the foot of the blanket just as Beth was picking up the baby and tucking Elizabeth's head into her shoulder.

"She's very active now," Laura smiled. "That's good."

"Is it?" Beth replied with relief and a hint of anxiety. "She seems so tiny, I can't help but worry about her."

"Only God knows how she will do. We'll do the best we can for her."

Beth kissed the crown of Elizabeth's head, then bit her own lip.

"You do know, Laura, that we can leave any time. We never meant to stay this long, and we don't want to be a burden to you."

I didn't expect Beth to say it at this moment, but I was indeed thinking the same thing. What was supposed to be a few days at most had turned into a few weeks, and it seemed that we weren't going anywhere. Of course, it was risky for Beth to leave with her baby so young, and Laura had said so herself before, but me? What was I even doing here? I could leave anytime; I had nowhere to go, but I didn't belong here, either. Laura was probably just too polite to kick me out.

"Don't even say such things. Of course you are welcome. Do you think I would turn you out when you and your baby have nowhere to go?"

"Well, no, but you really don't have to house us here."

"Yes, I do," she said, and there were no more questions about it.

She glanced at me, too, for good measure, and I hoped it was her way of reminding me that I was still welcome, too, but I wasn't sure.

Laura had two cows, a pig, and a small vegetable garden. Everything we ate came from the garden, which was relatively bountiful but not meant to feed three and definitely not suited for it, and the cows and the pig ate much and were of little use. Unless, of course, we were to slaughter them, which Laura was unwilling to do except in dire circumstances. Eventually, she decided to bring the pig to town to be delivered to the butcher or traded for something more useful. She didn't specify what exactly she thought would be more useful than the meat of a whole pig.

Our hostess decided to take me with her to town, which I was not terribly excited about, but I politely agreed and the next morning we bid Beth and the baby good-day.

The walk was a few miles, hardly an hour, and comfortably silent. On the way, we passed a long row of cotton fields, every bit of land dotted white, and I stared the whole time it was in sight. I'd never seen such a large farm before, neither had I seen planted cotton.

"My husband used to work there," Laura said.

"In the fields?"

"Sometimes I forget you're a Yankee." She chuckled. "No, only the slaves work in the fields. Johnny was an overseer."

"Oh," I replied, and, surprised by the taste of so many words on my tongue, continued, "um, what exactly is that?"

"He was in charge of making sure the slaves did their work and giving them what they deserved when they disobeyed."

"He whipped them?"

She ignored my shock and nodded casually.

"But not as much as Mr. Clay preferred. Johnny was fired for being too soft with them, and that's why he went to the army." The pig, which Laura was holding by a thick rope, snorted. "If not for that damned old Mr. Clay, Johnny would still be here."

I did not know whether her husband was dead or simply still at war, but it seemed an improper question to ask. It was difficult to comprehend that her husband had been an overseer; well, it was difficult to imagine slavery at all. I knew so little about it. Were the slaves whipped all the time? What were they whipped for? Was it very much whipping? In my time as a nurse, we'd had a few men come in from the post—there was that incident with Joshua, of course—with their backs raw with blood. It was an awful sight, and a few nurses had to take a whiff of smelling salt to keep themselves from fainting. Was this the life of a slave? And was it so painfully unjust?

The cotton fields gradually shrank from our view. Perhaps I didn't need to know anything more about the institution. It would go on as it had for generations or it would not. My knowing about the real experience wouldn't change a thing.

"Laura," I said, once we had reached a certain point in the road. "If you'll allow me, I need to stop here for a moment."

She raised an eyebrow but nodded.

I ducked between the trees, certain that this was the spot because of a tree that I had marked with an X. Sure enough, several paces deeper into the woods, he was exactly where I had left him.

He was still covered by a thin film of dirt, enough that no part of him was visible. This was not a vivid nightmare or an awful dream; this was real, right in front of me, here.

I fell to my knees.

I heard the scratch of twigs behind me, ever so quiet, but I did not turn my head to look. From the sound of soft breathing, I guessed it must be Laura. If it was not, if it was some woodland bandit about to slit my throat, then by God, let him do it. I didn't care.

After some time, I felt Laura's presence behind me. I had been weeping, so she noticed the wetness in my eyes.

"Your brother?" she asked softly.

I nodded almost imperceptibly.

"I'm so sorry."

I rose and turned back to her, and before anything else, she wrapped me in a brief, warm hug.

"He died honorably," she said. "He was a brave man."

It was then that I realized what a blessing she was to us, this wise, older woman—not only because she had taken us in for these weeks and helped us immeasurably, but because she understood. Of all the Southern women—in this town, for example—who else would have taken in two Yankee women and treated them like daughters without question? Who else would have given up her food so that a Northern baby might eat? Who else would have spoken such kind words for my brother, the Union soldier?

As we began to walk back, I whispered, "Thank you, Laura. Thank you for everything."

She gave a one-word response if any at all, but as we retrieved the pig from its haphazard confinement to a tree, I knew she really meant it. It was one of the few things I could say I was grateful for these days.

Chapter Nine

Beth was rocking the wailing baby to sleep. She'd been fussy as ever the past few days. I thought perhaps it was normal for an infant and that I didn't know anything at all, but little Elizabeth seemed unhappier than usual. In Beth's cradled arms, she looked so frail and tiny.

I entered the kitchen quietly, hoping to be of help to Laura. Hanging around the living room with Beth and the crying child would be of no use. I followed Laura out the door to tend to the garden, and once we were elbow-deep in potatoes and carrots and were still able to hear the infant wails, she spoke.

"I'm not sure about her," she said, almost to herself.

"What do you mean?"

"She should be bigger by now. There's little hope for a child that small. And hear how she cries—she is always hungry, but we have little to feed her."

"You think she will not live?"

She said it like a whisper, "I would not hope for it." She continued pulling carrots, then sighed. "If only there were more we could do. I'm trying to give her everything she needs, but I have nothing. I would have food if not for this godforsaken war. My husband would be home, and I would have his wages to pay for things, and that baby would not be crying so dearly."

I wiped the dirt from my hands onto my skirt. She was right; there were many awful things. Beth's baby would not be starving and fatherless, we would have food to eat, and Joshua would still be here. But then, we wouldn't be here otherwise. Surely, Beth would have had a child before long without the war, but not Elizabeth, and we would never have met Laura. But though Laura was the kindest of women, it wasn't worth it. There were plenty of kind women in the world; I would sooner have Joshua by my side. I was sure she was thinking the same thing: she would rather have her husband by her side than care for us, however kind she was about it.

"Beth will be destroyed if that baby does not live," I said quietly. "It's the only thing she has left."

Laura shrugged solemnly.

"It shall live if God wishes it to. But if He doesn't, there's nothing we can do."

I knew that, of course, but it stirred an uneasiness in my stomach. Of course I knew that babies were likely to perish, especially when there was nothing to eat, but it had never occurred to me that Elizabeth might not live through this. We were here, in this secessionist town, accepting hospitality from a kind old woman to take care of her. Why would she not live when we gave so much for her?

"Then I suppose we shall pray every night," I replied. "Day and night, we'll pray for them."

Laura nodded unconvincingly. To her, it seemed, there was no hope anyway.

Upon our return indoors, I stopped to watch Beth and the baby. Beth was leaning over the child, doing something to elicit the kind of laughter so hysterical that I was unsure whether the baby was laughing or crying. I watched the pair a long time; they seemed so happy. There were so many reasons for despair, reasons that neither of them could even know, and yet they played here, a small beacon of goodness in the midst of all this misery.

But what if Laura was right? What if the baby would not live?

Beth glanced up at me. "Come sit," she said.

I raised an eyebrow but complied, unable to think of a way to refuse.

"You should say hello." Beth smiled. "She'll like it if you say hello."

There was something distinctly uncomfortable about this. I didn't want to be here with this frail little child and the mother who was fragile in a quite different way. I didn't want to watch them.

"Here," I said, in a soft, awkward voice, a half-attempt at the squeaky, loving tone Beth used.

"Stick out your finger, she'll grab it."

Sure enough, the tiny girl wrapped her fingers around mine.

"She's so sweet," I said.

Beth had a faraway look.

"Elizabeth helps me a lot," she said distantly. "Sometimes I think she is the only thing saving me from madness."

A bird squawked outside the window.

I smiled emptily. "I'm glad you have her."

The baby giggled, soft cheeks flushed rose. I tried to keep Laura's words out of my head.

It started with a cough. Nothing really at first, but then Laura started to grow anxious about it, while Beth pretended nothing was amiss. I felt like an intruder, I made the motions of helping and being concerned, but I could feel nothing. I was not afraid the way they were.

We all prayed day and night. Laura administered some of her old medicines, assuring Beth that they would help but glancing at me with doubtful eyes. I hoped the child recovered, I really did, but there was a nagging voice in the back of my head: *"So many lost, what is one more?"*

I did my best to repress it.

"I suppose we must tell her at some point," Laura said, "if the child will not live."

"Do you now suspect that?"

She was silent. "We will continue to pray."

Two days later, to the sound of the infant weeping, we began to prepare for the worst. It was a slow fade, over several days, deteriorating from shrieking wails to low whimpers, the sound of losing hope.

Once, when the child was asleep, I heard Beth praying.

"God, please," she whispered. "Do not take her for Your own. Let me have her just a little longer. Just a little longer."

And then, I was sure, came the weeping.

Next morning, Elizabeth did not wake.

I expected Beth's wails to echo throughout the house, and they did, for a time. But her grief quickly became quieter, as if she had truly known all along that the child was not to be. Somehow, that was even sadder to see.

We buried her at the foot of a fledgling pine tree in the backyard. There was no gravestone, for we did not have marble nor anyone to carve it, but using one of Laura's kitchen knives, I was able to carve a small cross into the tree and a small *E* for Elizabeth below it.

Laura said the prayer. Beth was too overcome, and I hardly spoke these days, so it made sense—and besides, we knew somehow that Laura was more than familiar with burials. At the end of it, the three of us held hands in silence, kneeling over the small mound. It was a long moment, quiet except for the distant chirp of birds and rustle of leaves, and the rest of the world felt far away. Every overwhelming thing, every feeling of emptiness, seemed so insignificant. We were alone among the trees and the birds, and although there was an undeniable loneliness, it was comforting. Although we had lost everything, it seemed briefly that maybe everything would be okay. For a moment, I was free of the churning grief and the spiraling desire for revenge. But it was only for a moment.

"Amen," Laura said finally, and we wiped the dirt from our hands.

After about a week of grieving, Beth and I were forced to face the truth: we had to go. Laura had been too kind to us, and she probably would have let us stay forever if we wanted, but we didn't belong here. We didn't belong in this Southern town among the wives of those who had taken our men from us. We had to find our own way soon, and it occurred to me that maybe, wherever I decided to run to, Beth didn't want to come with me.

On Sunday, we went to church with Laura. We had gone a few times before, excepting one day when Beth was still recovering from the birth, and done our best to blend in with the small crowd. Everybody knew everybody, so there were questions about us, but Laura told everyone that we were her cousins, and nobody doubted it. They didn't ask why we had come to her, and they didn't ask why we had an incurable sadness about us. The melancholy, at least, was not so unusual these days.

Today, there was a curious buzz in the crowd. There were whispers, whispers like "*godforsaken Yankees*" and "*God will lend His hand to us soon, you'll see.*" Something considerable had occurred in the war. Judging from the vitriol among these Secessionists, it must be something quite wonderful.

Someone pulled Laura aside.

"You heard the news? A Yankee victory in Pennsylvania. The biggest one yet. I heard we've lost ten thousand."

Ten thousand. But it was hard to say whether that was true. It could be that many of that number were simply missing or captured. Still, it was a victory that was hard to ignore. I glanced at Beth. We dared not smile about it in this place, but we knew how good this was.

"How awful," Laura said with polite indifference. "That is tragic to hear."

"But we'll get them back, Laura. You know we will."

And so the chatter continued. After the sermon, while Laura

was chatting with some other ladies, Beth and I walked the next door over to the post office—not for any reason particularly, but to avoid the crowd of strangers. Before we even walked inside, I spotted a paper nailed to the front wall: Soldiers Wanted.

"Look at this."

"An advertisement for the army?" She squinted and tried to read it. "Eleven dollars per month—that's a good sum. We could use money like that, couldn't we?" She laughed bitterly.

"Yes." I was thinking. "We could."

She raised an eyebrow. Apparently, she hadn't expected me to be so serious about it.

"I wonder if the Union army pays the same. We aren't far from the border of West Virginia."

Beth shifted. "We should go back."

The walk home with Laura was silent.

As Laura retired for the night, I whispered, "We have to leave soon, Beth."

My companion, in the dim candlelight, rubbed her forehead.

"Yes, I know we do. We could go to a city and try to get jobs in a factory. Richmond isn't too far, is it?"

"We'll starve in Richmond," I said resolutely. Everyone knew the rotten state of that city. "We'll have to go North. There will be food and jobs there, better than anywhere here."

"We could take a train to New York." She shrugged. "I don't know where we'd get the money, but it's possible."

"And what, work in a factory for the rest of our days?" She seemed to be searching for a reply, but I continued, "I think we should go to West Virginia. It can't be too far. I swear it must be less than six days walking."

"And you think we will find jobs in West Virginia?"

Silence.

"Cassie?"

"I have an idea," I said, "but you'll probably think it's nonsense."

She snorted.

"After everything that's happened in the past few months, I doubt there's anything I would consider nonsense."

I said the words carefully, for they were unfamiliar on my tongue.

"I think we should join the Union army."

"What?"

"I told you—"

"That's ridiculous. We can't do that."

"Why not? It pays well, and we both saw that it does. We could disguise ourselves. It wouldn't be too difficult." In fact, I had no idea how difficult it would really be.

"But why? Wouldn't it be easier to work at a factory in West Virginia where we're not risking our lives?"

"Beth, the Rebels took everything from us. Don't you want to get back at them?"

"It's a bad idea, Cassie, and you know it is."

"It's the only thing I can think of doing right now. Otherwise, where else will we go? What will we do?"

Beth sighed. "We'll think of something better."

The candlelight began to flicker out. A few minutes later, we were awash in awkward darkness. I couldn't believe that I was seriously considering it, or that I actually wanted to do it, but I had a feeling deep in my gut that I could do nothing else from here. Beth and I were lost souls, and I knew that the army was somewhere we could find home again, however tragic and harsh it might be. Why couldn't we just be nurses again? I wondered why Beth hadn't asked that herself. But we had patched up wounds long enough. I wanted to inflict them.

Hopefully, Beth would come with me. Even if she didn't, though, I knew my course. I would don the Yankee colors as Joshua had. I would fight for him.

I stayed awake through the night, watching my friend's slumbering figure, waiting.

Beth and I were picking carrots in the garden the next morning when she finally spoke to me.

"I think we'll go to West Virginia. We'll find something to do in Charleston, surely, or perhaps we can work in a shop."

I grabbed ahold of a stalk.

"Whether you come or not, I'm going to the army."

A soft sigh. "You can't. You'll be discovered."

"Not if I'm careful. Do you think it's never been done before? If I fight well and do as I'm told, nobody will pay much mind to my business."

"That's madness. What's wrong with you? Why won't you just come with me to Charleston instead of getting yourself into trouble?"

Oh, now she was mad. What right did she have? I was going to do as I pleased.

"It's trouble. I can't go to Charleston and work in some god-awful factory while war still rages on!"

"You were never so patriotic before," she accused.

"It's not about that. I have to fight for my brother."

"I don't fully understand you."

"Perhaps you never will. But do you not feel some urge to finish the battles that Nicholas cannot? Will you not fight the battles he would have fought, suffer the pains and hunger he would have suffered, kill the men he would have killed?"

"It will not make him come alive again," she said, almost

pouting.

"But if we continue in their paths, then they did not die for nothing."

Beth seemed seriously to be considering this.

"It's still wildly stupid," she said. "We could get caught. We could be injured."

I didn't care about the danger. The thought of losing an arm or being killed in battle didn't bother me the way it perhaps should have. I just wanted to go.

"I'm going to West Virginia. The closest town I can find, I will enlist. Are you coming with me or not?"

She bit her lip. "I—"

"I'll leave in a week. That should give me enough time to prepare. You have until then to decide."

I gathered my small pile of picked carrots and brought them inside, leaving Beth in the garden. It felt already like I was abandoning her.

It was time. In the past week, I had acquired some men's clothes. While snooping around, I had found Laura's husband's belongings. There had been two pairs of pants, too large but certainly better than nothing, and every night after Laura retired, I was at work, fashioning a shirt from an old curtain found in the same closet. I would be like a rugged sort of boy wearing these things, but that was fine. I was a poor farmer's boy, that was what I'd tell them. That my Pa had died and I had come to the army because I had nowhere else to go. If anyone asked why they'd never seen me before, if I lived nearby, I would have to make up some story or another, but the hard part would be getting there. We had no horses. We could walk, of course, though that would take longer. By Laura's estimate, it took three days on a horse. We would need at least six days on foot, and we'd have to camp along the way, somewhere in the forest in the territory of night-time bandits. It was no thing for a woman to do. We knew that we would be dressed as men—and hopefully armed somehow, too—but we couldn't tell Laura that. So, she was worried for us.

"Are you certain that you must go? I will happily keep you longer, at least until you can find some horses. It's much better than risking your lives on those roads."

We shook our heads. There were reasons we must go, reasons we could not say aloud, but Laura knew them.

On the day of our departure, she pulled one of the hunting rifles from the wall.

"Take this. It should protect you."

"Are you sure?" Beth asked. "You might need it here."

She shook her head.

"This is already loaded if I recall correctly, and I found a few extra cartridges." She uncurled her palm to offer them. "I can't tell you how well they'll work—my husband was always the one who handled the guns, obviously, but I hope it will be useful to you."

We thanked her graciously. There was a deep, abiding kindness in her eyes that sparkled with a pang of guilt. But we had to go. This was the only way we could survive.

Then, almost too quickly to believe, we hugged Laura, and we took our leave.

Chapter Ten

I did not ever expect my life to be easy; however, I did not at any point foresee myself fashioning a makeshift tent out of an old dress, petticoat, and all.

"This is perhaps the most absurd thing I've ever done," Beth declared, using a small stick to rip hers down one seam. We intended to hang them flat like blankets between two trees for shelter; that meant we didn't have any sort of blanket, but it would have to do. We spread out the petticoats to lie on.

It would be a cold, cold night.

I dearly hoped nobody stumbled upon us: two poorly disguised women, hair still long, ripping up dresses for shelter. At least when we changed garments, we'd scavenged the cloth to bind Beth's breasts. I had nothing much worth binding anyway, but I helped my companion, and the result was something to boast about.

It took an hour, perhaps, to hoist the damaged dresses the way we needed them. Hopefully, we wouldn't have to do this again; there were small towns along the path where we could stop for rest, but we didn't have any money and hardly anything to trade. We could offer to work for our lodging, but pausing for a few hours to sweep floors and boil cabbage would certainly delay us in our journey. So we would have to brave the wind and the cold for some days more. We had suffered worse. We just kept the rifle close, that was all.

The next five days, we marched on, stopping a few times at towns along the way to beg for food. We also hoped that a little luck—and somehow enough success—would get us through. Beth was good at spinning stories. She told the gruff general store owner about how we were on our way to live with a distant cousin after the sudden death of our father, how we were orphans now, and how we would do anything we possibly could for a little bit of hardtack, even though we didn't have a penny to pay for it. It was enough to get us a few bites (the store owner looked as if he would just as soon bite off his right arm as give us anything more). And this story, repeated several times to different benefactors, was a lie, but there was a truth in the essence of it: we *were* orphaned, we *were* lost, and we *were* hungry. The details didn't mean much.

"Are you sure about this?" I wanted to ask Beth several times. *"Are you really sure you want to do this with me?"*

But I wasn't sure if I wanted to hear the answer.

So, without hardly speaking to each other, we swept miles of the dusty road beneath our feet, scrambling toward a future even more frightening than our past.

We rolled into Marlinton, West Virginia, with dirty faces and scraggly clothing, probably looking as if we'd crawled out of a sewer. On our way to the post office, we received some odd looks but nothing to stop us on our way. Beth trotted behind me, more hesitant, across the dusty path and past the small assortment of stores.

The postman hardly looked at us when we entered.

"Sir," I announced, clearing my throat. "We'd like to enlist in the army."

He put down his pen and looked us, up and down.

"Who are you?"

"Caleb and Timothy Johnson, sir. Brothers."

"How old?"

We glanced at each other.

"Nineteen and eighteen, sir."

Beth was probably older, but we looked young for men. I had turned eighteen about a month ago if I was right that it was now September.

He leaned in, giving us a waft of his stench.

"Are you sure you're old enough?"

It wasn't clear which one of us he was addressing.

"Yes, sir, in God's name we swear it."

He leaned back.

"All right, then. Show me your teeth."

"Our teeth?" Beth asked, glancing at me.

"Yes, open your mouth and let me see."

"Why—"

"Are you interested in joining the army, sirs? Then open your mouth and let me see your teeth."

Confused, Beth and I obliged. The postman took one look and appeared satisfied.

"It's to make sure you have enough teeth to bite off a cartridge," he finally explained. "One top and one bottom on the same side." He pulled out a thick signature book. "Sign your names here."

The pen was thick and inky, but we were able to sign it fine. We carefully printed our newly constructed names, and when we filled out the column marked *Birthplace*, I hesitantly marked, *Charleston, West Virginia.* Nobody would care where we were born—at least not what we wrote in this book.

"You boys are lucky. A new company is shipping off in a week, and you'll be part of it. Don't get yourselves into trouble before then."

He nodded his head in farewell, and we trotted out with barely contained excitement.

"We did it, Cassie," Beth whispered, radiant with her chopped-off hair. "He didn't ask many questions! I thought he saw right through us just that once—" she trailed off with an expression closer to a smile than I had seen from her in weeks. And then, something more solemn. "I can't believe we're doing this."

"This is for Nicholas and Joshua," I reminded her gently. "And Elizabeth, too."

"It's not too late to go to Charleston, Cassie. We could make an honest living there."

"With our hair chopped off and our clothes in rags? They would take us for—"

"Okay, I understand." She sighed deeply. "We can do this, right? We'll make it through this."

"We don't have a choice now," I said it almost happily, but it sounded remorseful.

I hoped Beth didn't notice.

Only a few days later, we were off with the Fourth West Virginia Infantry. At our enlistment, we had been given caps with small insignias to represent our company; the symbols were so small they were hard to make out. Beth insisted it was an eagle, but I thought otherwise. Beth had been nervous signing her name—determined, but nervous. We'd spent the whole walk there practicing how to speak, and when the postman opened the book for her to sign and she said, "Thank you, sir," in a deep, husky voice, I almost laughed aloud.

And then we exited the building, and Beth was all sharp edges now—pointed elbows, knobby knees, a defined jaw—and we both laughed because we had done it, we were doing it, we were soldiers.

Beth laughed as she puffed a cloud of cigar smoke.

"I can't believe you've never done this before," George said.

He had been the first to befriend us. He was Virginian, of course; he had a Rebel brother whom he hoped never to see again if you were to believe him, but I didn't. Something about the way he said it.

Beth blew another cloud.

"Never had the occasion. My Ma always said they smelled rotten."

"Nonsense," he said, wincing as some of the smoke blew by him. "What about your Pa?"

She shrugged.

"He wasn't around to say a thing about it."

Silence after that.

"You sure you don't want one?" he asked me.

I was prepared to decline again.

"That's ever so kind of you, but..." But, I had no reason to say no. "Actually, I'll take one. Thank you."

He shrugged. "I pity you both that this is your first time."

"Won't be our last, will it?" Beth laughed just as I erupted into a fit of coughing.

"Just try again," George's companion, Martin, told me reassuringly as if that helped. "Ah, there ain't nothin' like tobacco. Good thing we're going to Georgia, ain't it? We can get our hands on some of the good stuff down there."

There had been rumors about us going to Georgia, but nothing was certain. They didn't tell us anything.

As George and Martin each lifted a cigar to their mouths, Beth asked, "Can't we just trade for it, though? I thought I heard something about some of our men trading hardtack to some nearby Rebels."

Martin snorted. "The fools traded tobacco for *hardtack*? God above, they must really be starvin'. That musta been a while ago besides. There ain't any Rebels near us, least none I heard of." Nearby, a fiddler began to play a vaguely familiar anthem.

Over the slight noise, George said, "Where did you boys say you're from, again?"

"Charleston," Beth answered easily. "Got nothin' to do there, so we enlisted."

I could only see the lie because I was looking closely for it. She was good at acting like we'd left nothing behind.

"I'm sure your Ma lost her steam, with the two of you leavin' at once."

Beth blew smoke.

"Nah, she came around. Said, that with so many mothers giving up their boys, who was she to keep us. She probably would've liked Caleb to stay, but we can't be separated, can we?"

I cleared my throat.

"That's right, we can't," I replied, trying to match the noticeable twang Beth had adopted. She'd had a slight accent before, but for some reason, it was more pronounced now.

After a bit of silence, I said, "So, here's to Georgia."

"If there's anything left of it when we're done." George laughed.

Just as I was about to drift to sleep that night in a tent of eight, Beth whispered nearly inaudibly but intended for me to hear, "I miss home."

I didn't know what *home* meant to her, for neither of us had really had a home in a long time, but I was nervous that she was having doubts now, when she had just been gaily chatting around the fire like any other. "Tell me a story about Nick." That would remind her why she was here. Unless she became morose—or worse, started to weep—but I didn't consider that until after.

"I can't tell a *whole story*," she whispered conspiratorially. "We're talking so quietly."

"Tell me the thing you loved most about him."

"Fine."

A little too loud: "His smile."

Someone kicked her in the shin, so we shut up.

A puff of smoke accompanied him as he sat down.

"Did you hear the news?"

"I can't say we have," I replied, glancing at Beth to see if she was even listening. "Is it something from the dailies? I've seen a few around here, but I didn't know if there was any big news."

"No. No," he said, sticking a cigar in his mouth and lighting it. "Those are the same old, same old. Lincoln is distraught, the Irish are stirring trouble, and Southerners are now using berry juice because there ain't any ink left. No, it's not that." He chuckled, then pointed across the river. "Look there. D'you see anything?"

It was difficult to see through the trees, but I caught a glimpse of movement. I couldn't pick out what it was.

"Those are the Rebels."

"Which means—"

"That with God's blessing, tomorrow will be a fateful day for those sorry bastards. In fact, there might be a skirmish tonight if they start firing our way."

Out of the corner of my eye, I saw Beth tense up.

I bit my lip.

"Tomorrow, then. We fight tomorrow."

I was already imagining it: a rifle at my shoulder, Rebel blood on my hands. Joshua would be proud.

"Oh, you'll be fine," he said. "We haven't had many casualties yet. We've lost twice as many to dysentery than to bullets."

I sniffed. "I'm not afraid," I insisted. It wasn't a lie; it wasn't. "I've been waiting for this."

Beth shoved her pen and paper to the side, apparently finished at last.

"Do you realize that neither you nor I even know how to hold a rifle?"

I hadn't expected her words to be so biting.

"And how's that my fault? It's not so hard, is it?"

George puffed smoke.

"You've never shot a rifle? God's blood."

He stood up and wiped the dirt off his pants.

"Go get them, I'll show you."

"You're going to show us how to shoot?"

"Well, is there anything else to do around here?"

It was true. Five minutes later, Beth and I were at George's side with our weapons. Beth had made a small fuss about finding the courier to deliver her letter, but that could be taken care of later.

"Are you ready?" He grinned, and we nodded, leading us away from camp. "We'll have to go a bit out of the way…If we go near the river, the Rebels will think we're gunning for them, and we'll have a goddamned mess on our hands."

At his curse, Beth flinched.

"So we'll go the other direction and hope there's nothing to hit."

We reached a decent clearing—well, it wasn't bigger than some others we'd passed, but George for some reason decided it was good enough. Perhaps because it was far enough away. Anyhow, we were surrounded by trees.

"Now," said George, "you both will have to take turns." He gestured to Beth. "Tim first. Take out a cartridge and rip it with your teeth."

Five minutes later, after a lecture that I was probably supposed to follow but didn't, Beth was aiming her first bullet at a tree just ahead.

George counted, "One, two—"

Just as he said *three*, a bullet pummeled into the tree's bark.

He whistled.

"Quite some beginner's luck."

But I saw the look in Beth's eyes; even if it was beginner's luck, she was going to make sure it kept happening.

Two, three, four. Beth ran out of gunpowder, hitting once more and missing twice, which was apparently a fairly impressive feat, especially for a first-timer.

"Those weak little arms are more useful than they look," George chuckled, poking Beth's bicep.

She stiffened.

"I believe it's my turn," I said.

I knew I would be foolishly unskilled, but I had enough anger in me to make up for it. I wouldn't give up in battle until I'd lost every limb, and maybe not even then.

I had no idea what I was doing as I shoved the gunpowder down the barrel and raised the gun to shoulder level, but George didn't seem to have the intention of explaining it to me. I held the gun up, aimed it at the tree, pretended I was staring straight into the eyes of the man who killed my brother, and fired.

"Almost," George shrugged. "Don't spend so much time on it. It's ready, aim, fire, no delay."

I tried it. The second bullet grazed the trunk. The third time, I hit the target.

Beth clapped and, in her normal voice: "Good—" She corrected herself, going deeper, "…work."

The fourth time, I couldn't stop thinking about the Rebels. The chances were low, but I could run into the men who killed Joshua and not even know it. I could fire a bullet right between his eyes and not be wiser. It had been several men together who had taken him captive, dragged him to that town, and sent him Heavenward; perhaps not one single man was responsible. There were many with blood on their hands.

"Caleb, fire!"

With sweaty palms, I gave the last. It was a bust.

George wiped his sleeves and gestured back to camp.

"It'll be harder when you're really out there because everybody's movin' about—it's right chaos. But the good news is that you're more likely to hit something, even if you don't know what you're hitting."

"Were you afraid, your first battle?" Beth asked.

He laughed.

"Was I afraid? I went in there feeling like a hero, and I came out with a bullet in my foot wondering if it'd all been a rotten nightmare. I still have the scar, actually, from that bullet." He shrugged. "You get used to it, though, you understand? At first, you're about to be sick, you're thinking about all the men out there, all the bodies. Then it becomes less personal—then it's not so bad."

"Really?" I asked. "It's that easy?"

He laughed. "In thought."

In our tent that night, Beth shivered beside me.

"We're really doing this, aren't we?"

I nodded. It was deathly quiet, and the other half-dozen men were snoring peacefully. "You'll do fine, Beth. You're a great shot."

"Tim," she said, and I frowned. "My name is Tim."

"Right. Anyway, you're a good shot. You've got nothing to be afraid of."

"What if I freeze up? All that blood, all the bodies—I don't know if I'll be able to handle it."

"They're trees, remember? Just trees."

She sighed. "Even George said it's not that simple."

I took her hand.

"I'll be right there with you. Okay? You won't ever be alone."

She squeezed my hand. "Okay."

The next morning, one of the men sniffed as the trumpets sounded for us to rise.

"Do you smell that?"

"No," someone replied.

"It smells like blood."

Then he laughed. I tried to ignore the shiver down my spine.

Chapter Eleven

Bang. My heart was racing. *Not me, not me, not me.* Someone screeched, and a horse squealed as if it was being murdered. What a funny thing: it probably was.

Two bullets whizzed by me. Words that George had spoken over coffee that morning sprang to mind: *It's chaos, and every second you think it will be the end, but somehow it's not.* He was right; I was still here. But there was a long day ahead.

Ducking behind a tree, I closed my eyes for an ever-so-brief second, longing for a break. But if anyone saw me lingering here, they would think I was a coward; besides, this was for Joshua. I had work to do. So I bit my tongue and loaded the rifle.

"Get!"

I had no idea what it meant. All around, people shouted words that had the potential to be coherent thoughts but were ultimately too short to comprehend.

I spun around with the rifle and began to aim. Twenty yards away, I saw a perfect target, and as I raised the rifle and closed one eye for a shot, I hesitated just as George had warned me. *This is for Joshua.* I felt a pang of memory, an image of him as a small boy looking up at me with watery eyes and a big smile. Then I focused and put my finger on the trigger.

Boom.

I jumped to the ground, praying the gun didn't backfire, as a bullet whizzed overhead. If I hadn't ducked, it would have killed me.

Beth appeared beside me. We'd matched in arm-in-arm and moved in and out of each other's presence in the chaos of it all. But now she was here, for seconds and maybe even minutes, and I felt infinitely stronger, even though she seemed terrified despite her apparent skill.

"Get!" someone shouted.

We ducked to the side, and a small grenade erupted in the place where we had just stood.

"God," Beth hissed. "Oh my God."

A few yards ahead, a man clutched his eye and fell forward, screaming as he offered himself to the hard ground. More screams, and not just yelps of pain: real, rough screams, like pigs being slaughtered, creatures struggling for their last breaths, the screams of night terrors. I knew Beth was shuddering as we turned back to the chaos and took our shots.

The whole thing felt surreal. It was hard to comprehend it all at once. The air was thick with shrieks and bullets, and there was no making sense of it all. There was only the pounding of my own heart, thumping to a certain beat: *Stay alive, stay alive, stay alive.* I understood what Joshua found so thrilling about it; there was something tantalizing about holding your balance on the edge of death, not knowing whether you would live to the next minute and then the sweet release when you did. It was beautiful, in a way; my pounding heart, the gray sky above us, the air ahead filled with fog and smoke, and me aiming my gun with my brother's name on my lips. Dark moments they were…but beautiful.

The Rebels' retreat began just after sunset. In the near-darkness, we watched the sea of defeated traitors recede as if it had only been a small inconvenience, an annoyance at best, lapping our shores like a tide before ebbing.

In that quiet, far away from me, Beth screamed.

I almost tripped over my own feet racing toward her.

"Cl—Tim," I shouted, panting.

Everything started to go blurry. She was fine, I was sure she must be—she had probably tripped over something. There were no more Rebels in the vicinity to do any harm—but what if she wasn't?

The other soldiers glanced questioningly at me as I passed them. Was I revealing myself? I had never thought of it, but maybe this desperation, this hysteria, was chiefly a female characteristic. Maybe none of them would ever do this for their comrades. Still, I did not have enough worry about it to stop running.

I knelt beside her—blood was pooled at her shoulder, but I could not tell how much or if it was still happening. If she was treated by the nurses, they would have to take her shirt off, which would blow our cover. God, this was bad.

Beth panted as she said, “Caleb.”

Then she closed her eyes and drifted off.

I heard the rasp of her voice before I saw her eyelashes flutter open.

“Caleb.”

“Oh, thank the Lord,” I breathed, momentarily removing the pressure from her chest.

I’d only just had time to move her somewhere secluded, where nobody would accidentally stumble across us in their victorious stroll back to the camp. I just needed time to figure out what was going on—how bad the wound was, how long I would need in order to treat it, and whether she would eventually need to be hospitalized. I didn’t know what I would do if her wounds were that bad; I didn’t have any supplies nor any time. If we didn’t show up at the camp with the others, we would be considered missing. Soon enough, they would call us deserters.

“Were you shot?” I examined her chest with my hands.

“I don’t feel much,” she replied, lifting a hand to her forehead. “Where are we?”

“Somewhere secluded. I’ll treat you myself if I can. It’ll be easier that way. No questions. But we haven’t much time.”

I pressed my hand into her torn-up sleeve. There was no new blood.

"It looks like your shoulder was grazed, nothing more. Thank the Lord."

"Are you sure?"

I nodded. "Can you move?"

She sat up unsteadily. "Apparently so." Rubbing her forehead, she laughed. "How lucky. I'm not ready to lose my life just yet."

"You seemed terrified out there," I thought as I agreed.

She hadn't seemed ready for this, or even committed to it, so I was left to wonder: why had she done it? Why had she followed me out here if she was so mortified of the whole affair?

Still sitting, Beth relaxed against my knee.

"Are you ready to go back?"

"Not yet," she sighed. "Perhaps we can relax for a few more minutes."

Happy to oblige, I nodded in agreement. She seemed so calm now, breathing steadily against me, and I wondered if I was wrong. Maybe her husband, Nick, had been enough incentive for her to come out here; maybe I was just being foolish thinking that there must be some other reason. The battle was a scary thing, after all. Probably it was more than she expected, and she had gotten a fright out of it. That was all. It didn't mean she hadn't truly wanted it.

The sun was low, and even so far away from camp, we could hear the distant sound of celebration. Fiddling, maybe, and singing. How nice it would be to take part in it, but I was content to be here with Beth, smelling her newly masculine scent: tobacco and sweat. I cleared my throat.

"Why did you enlist with me?"

She seemed taken aback by the question, but still she was calm.

"What do you mean? It's for the sake of my husband, God rest his soul."

My fingers drummed against my knee.

"No other reason then? Do you like it here? Do you enjoy

battle?"

"Of course I don't. It's awful."

I regretted my questions.

"But what else would I do?" She smiled sadly. "Toil away at some factory job for every waking hour when there is Rebel blood to be had?" She looked away. "Perhaps that doesn't make much sense."

"No, it does." I grinned. "I know exactly what you're talking about."

"Mostly, I did this for Nick, though."

It seemed like an afterthought, a lie.

I watched her. While milling about camp and on march, my eyes were glued to wherever she was. There were little things, like the way her right hip swayed slightly more than her left when she walked or how there was sometimes an ever-so-slight note of hysteria in her laugh as she chatted freely with the other soldiers—I watched every bit of this and tried to discover the things she would never say. Was she regretting this? Had she changed her mind?

Sherman had us tearing up the railroads. All day we hammered away, pulling up metal and twisting it into knots, in order to stop trains from coming to aid the Rebels. While sweat poured down our backs and we squinted in the unrelenting sunlight, the men chatted gaily, snorting, "Funny how I used to repair this stuff, and now we're tearing it down," and "Johnny, I bet these Rebels have never *seen* a train before. Why, they've hardly got one line for the whole county!"

I couldn't stop thinking about Joshua. How weak he would be here (indeed, I was hardly keeping up and doing my best to hide the fact), but he would have done his best to labor alongside the others. And how he would have loved to drive Georgia into the ground to save the Union. He would have been happy here, in his naive way, uprooting railroad tracks and laughing with the other men as if he was one of them.

Ah, there were times where I so longed to put a bullet through a Rebel's nose.

It was mostly peaceful after that until the negroes came.

It took me a while to recognize that they were singing in English. The accent down here was hard enough to understand sometimes—not that I ever heard it much, for we never really spoke with the Rebels—but there was something different about the sounds of these women. The tunes sounded familiar, but I could only pick out a few words, mostly "freedom," and "liberty." They were happier and more gracious than angels, with a small cluster of children behind each one of them, carrying baskets of clothes and food that I doubted had initially belonged to them. For all that I had been mourning a few minutes ago, from the songs of these people, from their cheery smiles, it was Heaven on earth.

"The Lord has blessed us today!" they cried as they passed us, and while a few of the men frowned, others waved back at them.

Beth made no response, and neither did I. I wasn't sure what to think about the whole thing. They were free now, that was all I knew. The citizens had deserted their homes when they got word that we were coming.

Later that night, I found Beth by the river, dipping a bloodstained rag into the cold water. She glanced at me, questioning, and I didn't want to admit that I'd been searching for her because I'd noticed her absence at camp, so I cleared my throat and said, "I was just taking a break from the chaos back there."

"Oh."

"Do you need help?"

She shrugged. I knew she knew how to do it herself, but it was easier to have one person holding the cloth, while the other scrubbed. I waded calf-deep into the water, having abandoned my shoes by the riverside and rolled up my trousers and prayed my clothes wouldn't get wet. I took the cloth, and she continued to scrub.

"I don't know what I'll say if someone else finds us."

"What, about the blood? Just say you cut yourself."

She rolled her eyes.

"I'm not a good enough liar to make up a whole story like that. If I said I cut myself, I would have to say where, and then I would have to explain why the cut was so bad that I lost all this blood, and where I got this bandage…"

"Where *did* you get the bandage?"

"I stole it from the hospital tent. What, you don't believe me? I was desperate! I knew this was coming."

"I believe you." I smiled gently. "I have another week, and I'll probably need to do the same."

"Well, you can borrow this if we ever wash all the blood out. It would save you from resorting to thievery."

From the corner of my eye, I caught a chipmunk dashing up a nearby tree.

"Come, we're almost done. See? If anyone comes and asks, there isn't enough blood on this rag for them to be suspicious about you cutting your leg on a fallen branch."

"But the water is all red."

She snorted and then laughed heartily.

"Okay, okay. But we're done now. If we leave quickly we won't be suspected of anything." I snorted, too. "Just one thing. Next time, wait until we go out to battle. It'll be less suspicious when everybody else is bleeding, too."

She swatted my arm with the back of her palm. Then she

sobered.

"This whole thing terrifies me. Every day I wish I could go back home, but something keeps me here. Something besides not wanting to be caught deserting—at least, I think."

"Is it the campfire songs?"

Every night, Reed Allen pulled out his banjo and picked to melodies sung by Lewis Jefferson, who was enthusiastic but had an awful voice. Sometimes, the other men would join in and make it a merry time, but sometimes it was just Lewis and Reed warbling awkwardly out of tune.

She swatted my arm again.

"If that were the only thing keeping me here, I would have run off long ago. No, I fight for Nick, and I fight for my country, too, I suppose, but I don't love it the way you do. It just feels like I don't have another choice."

I don't love it the way you do? What was that supposed to mean? Did she think I was a vengeful, bloodthirsty woman?

"I don't love it."

I tried to ignore how it felt bitter on my tongue.

"Of course," she said, and she didn't sound like she believed me, but she wasn't arguing with me, either. "That's not how I meant it to sound."

"What did you mean, then?"

"Nothing." She rolled the rag in her hands into a ball. "It's really nothing."

I wanted to believe her, but I knew what a lie sounded like, and that was it.

They came in droves, ragged dresses flapping in the gentle wind, eyes lit like torches.

"They must have heard the news," George commented. "They

must know that we're coming."

It stirred something deep in my chest. Of course, I was glad we were conquering Georgia, but seeing these women now homeless and the dirty, wide-eyed children who trotted behind them didn't offer me the enjoyment that staring down a uniformed Rebel did. The men had chosen to arm themselves and lay down their lives, and though I wouldn't put it past any of these women to pick up a rifle and have their way if they'd been given the opportunity, they had still done nothing wrong yet—if one was to disregard their traitorous beliefs.

Still, I kept my feelings about the matter to myself, and we marched on to Atlanta.

It was several hours before we faced down the city walls.

Beyond the lines of houses and apartments, factory buildings dominated the skyline, and various churches dotted the city. It was easy to see how it had once been a bustling, lively city. And now we would watch it burn.

Sherman sent a group of us out to evacuate the remaining citizens. They were mostly cavalry, but he singled out another few hundred of us on foot, including me. The others, as far as I knew, were getting torches. Before we left, each of our officers issued a stern warning against pillaging, citing some age-old and long-repeated order. The men mostly shrugged it off; I was not sure whether this meant that they were well-accustomed to hearing the order and following it or if it was more of a formality than anything. I wasn't interested in looting, but if I found a few valuables here and there to shove in my pockets—well, I would need them for money sometime. I decided to watch the others and judge for myself whether it was a risk worth taking, although all the citizens had probably fled with their valuables or buried them, so we weren't likely to be rolling in riches.

We wandered through the city. On the main road, we stopped to observe all the stores, knocking on them as well as the houses and demanding evacuation, though it yielded little result. Nobody was in the stores at a time like this unless they lived there. We passed a small theater, which advertised some kind of burlesque show that I had not expected to see so far south of the Mason-Dixon. A short little store proclaimed: Auction and Negro Sales, and one of the men beside me picked up a rock and lobbed it through the window, laughing.

"Down with this treachery, you bastards!"

I had half a mind to copy him. And what luck that I didn't, because as soon as I decided against it, an officer trotted forward on his horse and pointed a greasy finger at the perpetrator.

"You there! I saw that! One more time and I'll have you whipped, you hear? We're not animals here."

The soldier nodded solemnly.

"Yes, sir, I understand."

"Hurry up, boys. You're not gonna find many people here, so make it quick and start heading toward the houses in the east. And no funny business."

Without another word, the officer trotted off.

The soldier sniffed.

"What does it matter, anyway?" he snorted bitterly, perhaps at me. "It'll all burn anyhow."

He checked to see that the officer was out of sight and tossed another rock, but missed, probably on purpose.

I longed for Beth by my side. She was sent out here, too, but she'd been ordered to scout the north side, and I had to go across town to the south. It was lonely without her; there were a few men on the same street as I was, including the recent culprit, but we weren't very close to each other physically, and I didn't know any of them.

Once we reached the residential area, a few scraggly old women were coerced from their homes, one shouting profanely at us, "Devil curse you! God's wrath upon you for destroying our homes!"

It was little of note; as Sherman seemed to believe, war was awful. It was the nature of the thing. If some thousands of people lost their homes in order to preserve the Union, that was a worthy price. Every Rebel had spilled the blood of our nation in some way, and for that I hoped they would pay dearly.

"Old witch," one of the men muttered. Then, audibly, "Come on, miss, we haven't much time."

"You wouldn't dare start the fires while there's still a living person inside this city," she replied threateningly.

"Is that something you want to find out?"

He shoved her along. Eventually, she had to be restrained. It took three men to subdue her writhing, shouting figure.

Once the last ones were evacuated, the order was given: "Let it burn."

The flames erupted. It was mostly the factories and shops that were burned, though that wasn't to say that the houses didn't go up in flames. Even some churches collapsed in smoke. And those words kept tumbling in my brain: *Let it burn. Let it burn.* It was haunting and deeply satisfying.

Finally, Beth and I found each other, and we stood together on the outskirts of Atlanta and watched the whole city turn to smoke like a giant campfire. Destructive, but beautiful. Having done this, having conquered and torched Atlanta, it seemed impossible that we would be defeated. If we had come this far, we could do anything. God was on our side.

But then, I had thought the same thing so many nights ago; I had believed that my brother and Beth and her family would make it out alive. Some things I was wrong about.

"We'll win this war yet," Beth whispered, chuckling as the smoke puffed quietly into the air and created a thick fog over the countryside—a smoke signal for anyone nearby that hadn't yet fled. I hadn't thought that Beth really cared; I thought she was in this for revenge, like me, but perhaps, we were both doing it for other reasons now. I had never thought much about the Union before—Joshua had seemed to care about it much more than I ever did—but now that we had nothing left but our sorrows and the blood on our hands, it was nice to believe that we were working for another and more noble cause.

Still, when the night ended and we lay ourselves down to rest, it was not the Union I was thinking of. It was Joshua.

Chapter Twelve

"We simply don't have room for them," George said, nose turned up. "The general knows that. He'll make the right choice."

How patronizing: *the right choice*. As if he knew better than any of us. It was midday, and the field was dotted with cards and dice; Beth and I had been invited more than once to join a game, but we had both declined. Perhaps the men were growing suspicious of us now; we didn't indulge in many of the pleasantries they seemed to enjoy, but at worst, they thought we were simply awkward, strange. We hardly received any odd looks. Besides, we usually had George with us—which, oftentimes, was a good thing. Not so at the moment.

Beth sniffed. "They have nowhere else to go."

He snorted. "Your heart bleeds too much. If we let them in, it will just make things worse for the rest of us. What then? Will you starve so they may eat?"

"I would gladly give a portion of my food to save someone else's life."

George poked her.

"How soft! Are you sure you're not a woman?"

I tensed up, afraid she would panic, but she didn't even hesitate.

"They let me come to this goddamned place. What do you think?"

The curse word shocked me, but I supposed it helped to illustrate her point. She briskly continued her work of sewing a patch on the calf of her trousers—while she was wearing them, mind, and the way she twisted her leg looked incredibly uncomfortable.

"Anyway, Sherman would be stupid to turn the negroes away."

"Why?"

"Well, it's incredibly heartless. I say the President wouldn't like it."

"You don't know a thing about Lincoln."

"No, but he seems like a nice fellow, and everyone knows he's sympathetic to them."

"Are *you* sympathetic to them?"

"What's the harm in that?"

"There's no harm. I just don't understand it. It's like…well, I don't feel any particular love for my horse—when I still had one, that is. It's a living creature, and perhaps it has feelings, but not the same way we do."

By this point, I was incredibly uncomfortable, and Beth visibly felt the same. She sniffed, offended.

"You're saying the negroes don't have feelings the way we do?"

"How can they? They don't think on the same level. They're simple creatures as I'm sure you understand."

"Even so," Beth argued. "That doesn't mean they deserve to be left for dead."

George shrugged, and with that Beth stood up, bid a curt and vague farewell, and stormed off.

George looked at me with bewilderment.

"Why does he care so much about them? I wasn't being prejudiced, for God's sake. It's God's honest truth, isn't it?"

It wasn't a question.

I looked at her retreating figure, then back at George.

"I should probably follow him," I said quickly and did so.

Beth was fuming in some far-off area of the field. When I sat beside her, she blurted, "I'm sorry, but I could not listen to that drivel any longer."

I laughed uneasily. I had no opinion on the matter, and I gathered that this wasn't the best time to adopt one. Would it be so bad to sympathize with the negroes? It seemed to me that George was right that they were base creatures, but Beth was also right that they didn't deserve to starve.

The negroes did come into the camp, after all. They were the refugees from Atlanta and some of the other cities which were being abandoned in anticipation of our arrival. Not every negro who begged for refuge had been granted it, so I heard, because there were so many, but we took in the ones we could. Beth wasn't thrilled that we had to turn some away; had it been her choice, we would have taken in every soul until everyone's rations were reduced to three coffee beans and a bite of hardtack. Entire families filed into the camp, praising us as if we were their lords and saviors, singing familiar songs in heavy accents. They spoke in heavy accents, too. After a few hours of conversing with them, I felt that I was able to understand most of it, but it did feel like they had a language of their own.

"Oh, let me tell you how it used to be!" one was saying to a group of enraptured soldiers. "Once I was having the sick the night before, and I woke up the next morning feeling like someone was tearing me apart from the inside out. But I didn't get a break, you know, so I went out to the field as usual, but it was so painful I could barely walk. So Massa noticed me walking a bit slower than usual, and he sent me right back to Jonathan. I got my arm broken that time. Took a week to heal, and I got whipped a few more times after that for working slower than usual—you know, because I only had the one arm— but it healed after a few weeks. I still have some scars on my back from the whip, if you want to see."

The soldiers' eyes were wide, and they shook their heads at the request. It was shocking, how matter-of-factly he told the story; it was almost joyous. Perhaps it was the realization that those days were forever over, but it was jarring how little it seemed to affect him. Surely, he hadn't had *that* much time to accept how awful it had been?

Beth was nearly in tears after listening to stories like this. Everybody had one; there were countless groups in the camp, and for every dozen soldiers, there were half as many negro men sharing stories twice as gruesome as any that we had from the battle, and yet very few were bitter.

"We have the Lord above to watch over us," one said. "We always knew that someday He would deliver us, and now the day is come. What on His earth do we have to be angry about?"

It was in that moment that I decided how I felt about the negroes.

"Sometimes Laura Beene would steal sugar cubes from the parlor of the mistress when she was cleaning, only if she knew she could get away with it, of course. She sewed a pocket into her dress to hide them, and every week, we looked forward to sharing them when she brought them back. She could usually only take two or three at a time, so we would each get a little nibble, but it was the sweetest thing we ever got to taste. The only thing we ate was leftover beans and pork, you know? So we would mix a little water in it and make soup. I'd never tasted anything else until once, when I was a cook. I snuck a spoonful of the soup I was making and"—he sighed merrily—"my, my, it was like the Lord Himself had come down and blessed me with the fruits of Heaven. Six years I worked in that kitchen, and I'd never known how delicious the food was! I always smelled it, of course—it smelled right good—but it was nothing compared to the taste. After that, I always snuck little spoonfuls, and by God's blessing, I never got caught. I would have been caned until my back was broken if anyone found out, but they never did. Good thing the mistress was too particular to ever go into the kitchen. Don't you think?"

Astounding. Absolutely astounding it was, how awful life had been for these people. And would it honestly get better? They'd probably never opened a book in their lives, and what other skills did they have aside from the ones they'd learned as slaves? Where would they find work? But then, anything was better than slavery, wasn't it? And they must have believed it because they rejoiced like nothing I'd ever seen. When the time came for campfire songs, they were the loudest and most enthusiastic singers on God's earth. They surely drowned out bad campfire singer—that was certain.

A few days later, we had marched on from Atlanta. Most of us supposed that we were heading all the way to Savannah, but we never got any information, so it was all speculation. At the town of Rome, we began to prepare for battle, and as soon as the word got out, the negro men declared that they were ready to raise arms along with us.

Our captain looked absolutely bewildered by the request. The camp was large enough that even the dozen men who approached him were not even a fraction of the entire number around here, so it was hard to tell if there were droves of men suddenly volunteering or if it was just this small group. Either way, they were sent along to Sherman, and until later that night, that was all we heard of it.

When they came back and began to work alongside us, fetching water from the stream and pitching tents, we heard bits and pieces.

"He said that if we were ever captured, we would be killed like dogs," one was telling me and Beth as we all played a lazy game of cards. "Doesn't matter to us. We don't expect mercy."

"And he's letting you fight?"

"Well, there are hardly any guns for us, but he's gonna ask for extra supplies from the President, and we'll see what happens. Seems hopeful to me, but it'll take time."

"Wow," Beth marveled. "I suppose you'll all be working in the hospital for now, then?"

"Sure we will. And I don't know if we're really supposed to, but Lord knows if I see a man down in the field, nothing's gonna stop me from running in there to grab his rifle and continue his work."

Beth grinned, although it seemed a morbid thought to me. Oftentimes, we retrieved the jackets, trousers, and boots from our dead before we buried them—they were all wearing undergarments, so it wasn't as if we were stripping them naked—and the clothes would be reissued to new officers or given to those who needed new ones. Of course, "needed" was a very strong term—only if your garments were ripped to threads would you be granted the privilege of a replacement. And though very few, if any, men sewed their names onto their coats or anything of that sort. Oftentimes, one would reach into the pockets and find something that was not theirs—a pin or a button from the late owner. Sometimes, even a letter from a sweetheart. The letters were the hardest—it piqued their curiosity to read one if it was found, but to me, it felt like intruding, like I was prying on someone's intimate life without their permission.

Beth continued chatting with the negro man, and I kept glancing about—was it not a bit odd for her to be having a private conversation with him? Granted, nobody else knew she was a woman, and there was less risk for a man to be talking with this negro, but how would the others perceive it? I didn't know if I was comfortable with it. If the other men started to single her out or refused to associate with her because she was consorting with negroes, it would be bad for both of us.

It was probably nothing. The other soldiers were open-minded, and of course, in groups, they were more than happy to enjoy the company of the negroes. Still, it was cause for worry.

"You're not her guardian," I reminded myself. *"She can act on her own judgment."*

But, again, I couldn't let her mess things up for us.

She was laughing.

"Caleb!" she snorted, patting my arm.

I was fairly certain that she knew I hadn't been listening to their conversation.

"James was just telling me how he had a brother named Joshua, too. What a coincidence!"

Her voice was cautiously deep as always, careful not to reveal her true gender, but there was something in the way she spoke to James that edged on feminine. It would have made me nervous, except for the fact that Beth had said *had.* James *had* a brother named Joshua. I didn't want to hear about how the poor boy had been whipped until he passed out and never woke up, or how he had gotten his hand caught in some infernal agrarian machine and contracted a horrible infection and died. I couldn't handle any more tragic stories right now, especially because no matter how many I heard—and no matter how much worse they were—I couldn't seem to forget my own.

"How thrilling," I said hollowly. "I'm sorry, but I'm going to go down to the creek for a minute."

Beth's eyebrows knitted together.

"Why? What troubles you?"

"It's nothing," I replied, searching for an appropriate excuse but coming up empty. "Nothing."

I could probably have turned my fingers purple from dipping them in the creek—that's how cold it was—but I continued to swish them through the water, ignoring the pain until I didn't feel it anymore. Until I was numb. It was hard to comprehend that I'd lived on for almost a month now, inching my way through daily life without Joshua. Things almost felt normal now. Well, there was nothing normal about joining the army, but my days were nearly predictable again—we were either fighting, marching, drilling, or lounging about playing cards—and there were times where I would start to laugh at someone's joke, or we would be on march, and I would wipe sweat from my forehead and realize that I hadn't thought about him in an hour. Sometimes, I would go half a day without feeling like I was made entirely of glass, hollow on the inside and more fragile than a baby bird. Sometimes, I would take a deep breath after a long march in the sun and think, *"Maybe someday I'll be okay."*

It hurt. Because there was an ever-present part of me that secretly hoped I would never move on. Moving on seemed a lot like forgetting.

After not so long, Beth appeared beside me. I didn't notice her at first, not until she was there, and I realized I had heard her footsteps but been too distracted to pay attention.

"What troubles you?" she asked in just the same tone as she had back at the camp: soft, in a way that set me on edge because it was so different from the low growls and rowdy hollers of the other—well, of the men.

It didn't seem like the kind of thing I could properly argue about with Beth, but I knew we couldn't afford to be so gentle around each other.

And yet we were, and nobody cared. They were all too busy with each other. Maybe, if someone decided to be a right menace, he would start bothering us, but it hadn't happened so far.

"Nothing," I repeated, just as I had said before.

She sighed. "You know that's not the answer I'm looking for."

"What if I don't care what answer you're looking for? Who are you to tell me?"

I stopped, because I knew I was more controlling—in my head, at least—than Beth ever was.

She smiled and shoved me a little. "Of course I won't make you tell me. But whatever it is, I probably understand."

She probably did. She'd lost her husband, after all. However, she didn't seem all that affected. I didn't doubt that she had grieved well, or that she still missed him, but she seemed as if she were moving on. Or at least on her way there. But what did I know? Maybe it was eating her up inside, and she simply wasn't showing it. She did have that air about her—a certain elegance and class that made her seem emotionless sometimes. It wasn't as if I always showed my grief either, but unlike Beth, I could be found staring off, in a somber way, into the distance sometimes, always retreating back to a default sadness. Anyone looking closely could probably notice. Beth, however, always looked utterly and completely normal.

A small fish leaped from the water, suspending itself in the air for just a moment before it fell.

I didn't want to talk about this. If we were to be men here, we couldn't sit about discussing our grief. Maybe if we were back home with Elizabeth, we would talk about it all day, relay tales of our beloved lost ones. Here, we rubbed dirt on our cheeks to mimic stubble and chatted in low tones along with the others. We gambled and chortled along to bawdy tales that would've made our mothers weep with astonishment. We were soldiers.

So instead of spilling tears, I peddled lies.

"It's nothing, I swear it. We've got quite a day tomorrow, and we should rest for it."

At first, I thought she would not follow me back to the camp. Then, along with the rustle of trees and the low hum of crickets, her footsteps crunched the twiggy earth. This time, I wasn't too distracted to listen.

I had just bitten open another cartridge when I saw the first negro on the field. My heart fluttered at the sight—was it pride that we had a few extra reinforcements or anxiousness for the twofold danger he was subjecting himself to? No time to think about it. Ready, aim, shoot, and I sent another bullet flying. The sight of blood was rewarding.

But the negro—he was ferocious. He was loading at twice my

speed—I calculated—and shooting with impeccable accuracy. Every third bullet hit its mark. The truth was, when a dozen or so others scattered onto the field, they were the same. I wondered why—they'd had no training, and it wasn't as if they learned the art of shooting when they were enslaved, unless I was vastly mistaken about the workings of cotton plantations.

A bullet whizzed by me, missing by half a foot, and behind me a comrade gasped. Well, it had hit a mark. My instinct was to rush back and help him, but protocol demanded that I not so much as look back. *Keep moving forward, keep moving forward.* Just like in drills: one step left, one step right. Do not turn back. Do not stop to think about what you're doing.

But, of course, I did that all the time. If I wasn't always thinking about what I was doing, I *would* turn back. Some of the other men were as precise as factory machines— ready, aim, fire; ready, aim, fire—as if they were made of little metal pieces instead of flesh and bone, as if they were just being cranked along. Maybe they were more accurate than I was, but I had something they didn't. A machine, if broken, could not simply put itself back together. Me? I searched for the fear in a man's eyes before I aimed a bullet between them, and if I fell, it was these memories that brought me back to my feet. A machine could easily break, but I didn't. I couldn't.

Suddenly, I realized about the negroes. Perhaps it wasn't skill or experience that made them so talented; perhaps it was because they had so much more to lose. This battle, if lost, would more than certainly be deadly for them the way it wasn't for the rest of us; in God's name, they had their freedom to gain in this war.

Bang. I was chuckling to myself as I pulled the trigger; how petty my revenge spree now seemed. And yet, I wasn't ashamed of it. Everyone had their own reasons for being here, for doing this. Maybe others were more noble than mine, but it was no matter.

Just in front of me, a man fell to his knees. I couldn't see what had happened until I stepped over his crouched figure, and then a pool of blood was more than visible. In a quieter corner of the field, nearing the end of the battle, three Rebels—officers, likely—knelt with their heads bent. One by one, they were shot through the skull. It was an odd incident; usually people were kept alive upon capture. Maybe they'd refused to surrender, or tried too hard to fight back. Still, it chilled my heart.

Until it didn't. Until it was just like everything else here: rough, but not too much to comprehend. I was numb now; no, not numb—I was thriving. The battle made me feel alive.

Joshua came to me that day. Not in body, and hardly even in spirit, but little memories of him flitted through my mind. Some moments. It was like he was really with me—as a little boy, presenting a small flower and saying, *"This is for you, Caddy"* or as an older boy with fire in his eyes as he spoke of the Union like it was some coveted ideal. I heard words that he'd never spoken in life but would have if he were here: *"We shoot for glory, and victory, and freedom."* The kind of words you can only say when you're young and strung up with hope, when you haven't known much of the world. These moments were what I lived for, and I only found them in the thick of the battle.

I supposed I was like a machine sometimes, the way my mind wandered but my hands still moved as they ought, but I was different, wasn't I? I did it for different reasons.

Ah, what did it matter? As long as the bullets hit their mark, everything else was just nonsense.

Chapter Thirteen

The Georgian city of Rome was burned in a day, and after the fall of Atlanta, there wasn't much of the event to make note of. People fled, buildings burned, and we left in a lingering cloud of smoke. Beth participated in the whole thing with a stiff air, and I watched with hungry eyes as the flames torched Rebel homes.

Then, on the road, we found *her*.

There were some stragglers on the path, mostly from cities we hadn't reached yet—the ones from Atlanta and Rome headed west, away from our path. It was a day as hot as the sun without the mercy of a breeze, and the first sign was a spray of pebbles.

At first, we thought nothing of it. It wasn't unusual, with all the kicked-up dust, to be hit with a few pebbles, but it happened for such a time that we craned our heads to look.

"In God's name," someone cursed, "see that girl throwing rocks."

At first, I doubted whether he was serious, but sure enough there she was, scrambling to find rocks and hurling them with an almost feral look on her face. Some of the other men laughed at her as she screamed profanities, hurling laughably small rocks our way.

Since Beth and I were enlisted with the same last name, we marched next to each other in the loosely-alphabetical marching line. I saw her glance back at the wild young woman, but she didn't say a word. Although we were far back enough, and it was fair to whisper a bit without being caught, she was paranoid about being overheard by the people behind us with the supplies train and of course, the handful of officers in the back. Thus it was that I felt an odd pulse of sympathy for this deranged creature of a woman and wanted to say a few words to Beth about it. I could do nothing but stay in step, counting *one, two, one, two* as if nothing was amiss.

However, it was only a few minutes later that we stopped for camp; it made sense when I noticed it was near dusk. After a few hours, we were all set up, and most people at the camp were engaged in evening leisure. Beth and I were involved in a rowdy discussion about trading with the Rebels for tobacco.

"There is nothing on this earth worth consorting with our enemy for," someone hissed, to which another replied, "Well, we're going to beat them to the ground no matter what, ain't we? Might as well get some goddamn tobacco, too."

I tugged Beth's arm. "I'll be back before dark."

"Where are you going?"

I shrugged. I didn't have a good excuse, and I didn't want to make one up.

"Come with me, and I'll show you."

I didn't have to look behind me to know she was following me. The good thing about not participating much in the camp leisure was that it was easy to slip out without being noticed. The captain usually only did roll call before the battle and drills, so he wouldn't be looking for us.

"Where *are* we going?" she asked once we were out of earshot.

Biting my lip, I replied, "I just want to see if I can find someone."

"*Find* someone?" She gasped. "You mean that mad woman we saw today?"

"She can't be too far."

Beth huffed. "And what exactly are you planning to say to her?"

"I don't know yet."

Beth pouted. The faded sky blue of her uniform had grown dirty, giving her a rugged appearance that was strikingly different from the woman I had first known as a nurse. Back then, she looked the sort of woman who faced hardship with resignation and hope. Now, her strength was in the form of steely indifference and something that I hesitated to call rage.

I wondered if I'd changed as much as she had.

The day fell in a parade of bright colors—a sunset that illuminated our search for this crazy woman. Beth was visibly frustrated. Truly, I had no idea what I was going to tell this woman. Would she even listen to me?

A more pressing question that I could not answer: what did I want from her? The chance to express my sympathy or to ask questions. Did I want answers?

It was a long walk, not assuaged by the not-so-subtly annoyed Beth.

When we were small, Joshua once wandered off into the lush escape of trees behind our home. I remembered looking for him for hours, screaming his name until my throat was raw, and minutes before I was about to trot back home to Ma and admit defeat, I spotted him carving letters onto a tree with a sharp stick. This, right now, felt a lot like those moments when I was searching—those moments when I wondered if it was hopeless. Though, of course, with Joshua I never doubted that I would find him, because I would do whatever it took.

After a quarter-hour of searching, we heard a distinct crackle of leaves, and there was she, sitting beneath a tree, curled up like a small child—hands around her knees, head turned down. It was downright pathetic.

"Well," said Beth, "here she is if you've got something to say."

I was unsure, but with Beth judging me so fiercely, I did not take the luxury of hesitation.

"Excuse me," I said squatting beside the infantile woman.

She jerked her head at me and regarded me so hatefully that I wished I were in my old nurse's garb instead of the harsh uniform I had now. And I had to act as a man, too, which made me markedly less sympathetic.

"What? Have you come to take the last of what is mine?

Because I have nothing left."

"No," I replied quickly. "No, I have not come to harm you. I've come to…to ask you to join us."

Her eyes widened but only for a moment before her face hardened again.

"I know not what you mean."

"A nurse," I suggested. "You can be a nurse and help treat us soldiers."

She wiped her hands on her dress.

"You all must really be down and out if you're recruiting aid from your victims."

Her venomous glare did not cease.

This had been a fool's hope. What did I have to say to this woman? How could I possibly convince her? Then, Beth did something that made me adore her evermore.

She stepped forward and asked, "What is your name?"

The woman, whose legs were now flat on the ground, now crossed her skinny, dirty arms.

"You should leave me alone."

Her eyes darted between Beth and me, and none of us moved a muscle.

"Katherine," she huffed. "I am Katherine."

She could not have been older than sixteen, I noticed. Hardly a woman yet, and somehow she had seemed so much older before. Perhaps because she was alone.

"I'm Tim," Beth offered kindly, so much like a mother. "And this is Caleb. We want to help you."

"Yes," she said as she sniffed sardonically. "I'm sure that's true."

She turned away from us as if to ignore us. The young girl *was* ignoring us, no question about that, but I knew that if she truly wanted us to leave, she would have left or at least pushed us to go.

Apparently, Beth knew this, too.

"Katherine, you may not believe us, but we really do want to help you. We understand that you probably lost your home—"

She snorted.

"Yes. Because of you!"

I could have launched into an impassioned speech about the politics of the thing— or at least my side of it: how we were only doing what we were told, and we wouldn't be here if not for the godforsaken Rebels anyway, but it was too much. She could never know how this all was so much more than just soldiers burning her town. I told her in an effortlessly sympathetic voice, "But Katherine, we've had losses, too."

Katherine frowned disbelievingly. Yes, she probably thought we were being superficial. Maybe we were talking generally, as in, our regiment had suffered some losses, or maybe we were just lying. But we weren't.

The sky thundered. Judging by the clouds above, it would rain soon, leaving Katherine without shelter. She glanced nervously at the sky, apparently thinking the same. There had to be some way to convince her to come with us. What did she want? Revenge? Comfort? I could not offer those. When Joshua died, I would not have listened to the words of a Rebel soldier for comfort, that was for sure. I would sooner have clawed his eyes out. What could he have offered me?

The sky cracked like a whip. Perhaps I was overthinking this. Shelter, food—surely, she was in need of those. I patted her on the leg. She jerked away, but no matter.

"If you come back with us, we'll give you rations and a place to sleep away from the storm. Will you do it?"

She averted her eyes, and I knew her struggle—I could feel it. Succumb to the enemy or die. It wasn't as if we were threatening to kill her—we weren't—but she knew as well as we did that she would have quite a time surviving on her own. This girl, in her torn-up dress and dirt-stained skin—I understood her, because maybe, if things had gone differently, I would have had to make her choice. I probably would've chosen wrong.

She wouldn't, though. I knew she wouldn't.

Beth coughed.

"It's near dark. We should go."

"One moment."

I addressed Katherine once more.

"This is your last chance. Food and shelter. Come with us now."

She shook her head slowly, not like a refusal, but like she didn't know what to say. We waited a long moment for her to respond, and I would have waited all night, but when Beth pulled my arm, I scampered behind her back to the camp—back home.

Only after we were several strides away, did Katherine do as I knew she would. We heard the rustling footsteps behind us, and then there she was, this girl who could have been my twin, following us to her new home.

The truth of the matter was that I didn't know what they would do with Katherine. They would accept her as a nurse, no doubt—it was to the point where they'd take in anyone with two hands, and their training was as simple as learning how to bandage a leg wound and when to call the physician for an amputation. The problem was that I didn't know if they would have enough rations to offer her. I prayed that they would; if not, I would have to offer her some of mine, and it wasn't as if we were given bucketloads. We would survive, sure, but we'd be hungry. I supposed that was better than letting Katherine starve.

I didn't tell her any of this, though. She would get food somehow.

The young woman shuffled behind me as we entered the

hospital tent. She looked so ragged that I wanted to assure her that she would receive a uniform when she was trained, but this as well as the rations, I doubted. So I patted her shoulder as I pressed the tent flaps open, regretting the gesture immediately by the way she shied from me.

I was familiar with a few of the nurses—I knew their first names, at least—so they smiled warmly at me as they tended to the reclining injured. They probably assumed I was just here to visit someone because they did not halt their work to address me.

Katherine looked petrified. Oh, Lord, and this wasn't even the worst of it. How would she hold someone's leg down for an amputation if she was fazed by a few bandaged legs and some dysentery?

I cleared my throat.

"Jane," I addressed the nurse nearest to us, who appeared to be taking a momentary break. "This is Katherine. She'd like to enlist as a nurse."

She scanned Katherine up and down.

"You'd have to talk to Captain about that."

"I know," I lied. It should have been obvious, though, really. "I just thought you might want her to start helping while I sort things out with the captain."

"Is she trained?"

I glanced at Katherine.

"No," she said.

Jane shrugged.

"God's pity on me that I'm not surprised," she muttered.

As I exited the tent after a brief farewell, I heard Jane give curt but friendly instructions.

"I'll have you follow me and watch. You'll have to learn how to bandage, at least, but that's for later…"

The captain's tent was scattered with papers—maps and letters, as far as I could tell. He was conversing with a black-haired orderly, a knot between his brows, and when after a few tense moments, the orderly scampered out with a few visible beads of sweat on his forehead, I opened the tent flaps and invited myself in.

"What?" the captain barked.

My heart was galloping. His eyes were small, beady, and crazy. There was something quite unstable about the way he looked at me.

I cleared my throat.

"I've found a young woman who wants to join as a nurse."

My shoulders were squared, and my chin was up, a posture I would never have assumed if I were wearing a dress; I was mimicking the behavior of other soldiers. The way the captain's gaze bored into me, though, tempted me to shrink down and break eye contact as the woman in me would have done.

"I want to make sure there are rations for her."

I wondered for a moment if it was a mistake not to bring her here, but she wouldn't have to sign her name anywhere if things still worked as I remembered from my days as a nurse, and I knew that—if anything—procedure had not gotten *more* strict. However, the captain would most likely want proof of her existence if he was going to have rations doled out for her. I hadn't thought of that.

The captain sighed as if I had done him ill.

"We have dozens upon dozens of negroes stinking up this place."

I bit my lip thinking how Beth would be blowing smoke from both ears at this statement.

He continued, "And not enough food for them. What makes you think we can feed another?"

"It doesn't need to be very much, sir, I can give her part of my ration—"

"And where is this young lady, besides?"

"She's already at the hospital, Captain, doing her duty."

"A duty that nobody ordered or authorized for her, yes?"

"That's correct, Captain."

"Then why should she receive compensation?"

This logic was beyond my comprehension. Just because she hadn't marched herself over here to beg permission before lifting a finger to help our soldiers, she didn't deserve to eat? I wondered who had promoted this wretched man. Captain Bradley started scratching away at a piece of parchment with his pen, and I thought he meant to ignore me until I left. Instead, he lifted his head just slightly.

"There's a price to pay for taking in strays," he said. "We have too many already."

I uttered not a word as I stormed from the captain's tent.

Without the courage yet to report to Katherine, I hunted down Beth. She was amid a crowd of rowdy card game spectators, and I cut through the thick group to reach her. Immediately, she retreated with me.

"Is there trouble?"

"The captain won't give her ration. We're going to have to feed her from our own."

Beth's eyes narrowed, and I realized I had misspoken.

"I mean to say, *I'll* feed her."

"Don't be crazy. I'll help, too."

She wiped her brow.

"How could he deny her?"

"We're already stretched thin, as I hear."

She shook her head, fuming. It was a good thing she didn't know of his comment about the negroes.

"So that's it, then? We have to give up our rations to feed her? All three of us will starve."

"No, we won't."

I wasn't quite sure of myself, but we couldn't lose hope.

"We'll find a way. We always have, haven't we?"

She looked doubtful about this.

Chapter Fourteen

For the next few weeks, Beth, Katherine, and I ate like birds, and not voluntarily. We were careful not to spend too much time with her because two soldiers in close relations with a nurse would arouse suspicion—or so Beth insisted, and I was so surprised to be on the other end of such an argument, that I went along with it—but we always made sure to drop some bread and coffee beans in her hands on our way around the campfire. I sensed that this did not satisfy her, but since she was eating more than both of us, she smartly kept her silence.

The day after Katherine's arrival gave her the true test: the Rebels mounted an attack at Griswoldville, and thus the bloodshed began.

It was a day like any other for us since we were so accustomed to battle. The Rebels swarmed in like ants—angry and mindless. Rifles puttered volleys every which way, and dozens of souls ascended to Heaven at once. The screams, by this time, were easy to ignore.

We marched back to camp sweating and satisfied: it was an easy victory. Apparently, Katherine did not see it that way. She emerged from the hospital with her arms clutched to her sides, dirt and blood on her dress, eyes wide and frightened. She looked as much like an abandoned child as she had on the first day we saw her.

Beth approached her quickly.

"Are you all right?"

She shook her head slowly.

"It's hard at first," Beth reassured her, "but you get used to it."

Katherine mumbled something.

"Do you want some food?" I asked. "We've got hardtack and beans."

With an expression that hinted she would rather eat live

worms, she nodded.

Beth and I sat next to her as she ate—not too close, of course—and watched her worriedly. It was a good thing, at least, that she was able to take a break from her work; if we had many casualties, the nurses had to stay in the hospital all night, but today the casualties were almost all on the Rebels. Neither Beth nor I pushed the young girl to say anything, but we both assumed that she would speak at least a few words that night. No, nothing. It looked like her soul had floated from her body and left her bleary-eyed and emotionless.

It was shock, I was certain, and I knew it would fade before too long—but would it? I, surely, hadn't been affected this much. It had been heartbreaking at first, to be sure, but war was part of life. The lion eats the lamb, and so on. Life wasn't all sunshine.

As the sky was darkening, I cleared my throat.

"Katherine. Do you want to talk about it?"

She shook her head, still looking quite soulless. I glanced at Beth, and she shrugged helplessly.

Well, Katherine would have to snap out of this mood sometime. Until then, the best we could do was pray.

It was on a Sunday, just after worship, that they came. Droves of prisoners, wretched and dirty men, with little soul left in their eyes. They scrambled in as the afternoon sun hooked its rays into the clearing between trees, disrupting the tranquility and happiness of a post-battle afternoon.

We didn't know they were prisoners, really, but someone muttered it as we caught the first glimpses of them. And what else could they have been? They were not citizens; they were hardly men. That they had been locked up and treated like animals until an escape which led them here—well, that made sense.

What would happen to them here? Unfair it would be if their appeals were successful when our captain had spared not a bite of food for Katherine; but then, these were soldiers, and they were appealing directly to the general. I could not imagine any of General Sherman's superiors—the President, namely—smiling upon a decision to turn away hundreds, maybe thousands of refugees, especially after we had taken in so many negroes. But we had been eating less than two meals a day for weeks now—these men were hundreds more than we could feed.

I knew what Beth was thinking: it is better we all be hungry than let one man starve. Yet, what if we were all starving?

"We'd have to turn out all of the goddamn negroes to feed this bunch," someone muttered.

Another said, "I hope we do. They've been stinking up this place for far too long."

"Captain says he wants to be rid of them, but Sherman won't let him. What a fool! I heard he even lets them into his house. *Speaks* to them, if you can believe it. He should be whipping the sense into them."

"Beth," I whispered. "Let's move somewhere else before this gets ugly."

"I'm fine," she said, but her eyes were gleaming with anger.

She was good at hiding it, though; it was only detectable in the slight stiffening of her posture, the pursing of her lips, the subtle narrowing of her eyes—little things. Beth still looked polite as ever.

Only a few minutes later, General Sherman trotted in on a giant strawberry roan to make an announcement.

"It is a pleasure to know that after all your miseries in prison, you have found yourselves safely here—" and thus began a diplomatic but terribly dull speech.

My mind started to drift.

It had been years since Joshua and I stood in a throng of

townspeople marching off like heroes. The bleat of trumpets, the sonorous, proud melodies—I could still hear them just as I could still feel the bright summer heat. I had not thought it a blessing, then, to go out as we did, but even my worst nightmares could not have predicted what was to come. My worst nightmares would not have put me here, with a gun in my hand and a hole in my heart, watching a small army of skeletal victims come into our ranks and having hardly the capacity to pity them. So, they had suffered—what difference did it make? Beth and Katherine had suffered. The negroes had suffered. Every man we peeled lifeless off the battlefield had suffered. *I* had suffered. Their pain could not be worse than ours.

"Thus," Sherman concluded at last, "we are pleased to welcome you back into our ranks."

When he said it like that, it seemed inevitable. *Of course* we would accept them; they were soldiers. Yet anyone who looked at them could tell that it would be many weeks before they could pick up a rifle again. We didn't have room for so many in our hospitals.

Somehow, then, we would have to make room.

I found her tending to some flesh wound on her negro friend, James. He was hunched over, shirtless, and she was pressing a cold cloth to the dark skin of his lower back, smiling as they chatted away.

"There is a hospital just over there," I commented as I sank into the grass beside them.

"Ah," James said in his unfamiliar accent, "but they are so full with the prisoners now that they won't treat small wounds like this."

I wanted to turn up my nose at them. They looked happy like old friends. It was uncomfortable to watch.

"Whenever you're done," I asked Beth, "can I speak to you in private?"

"You can speak to me now," she said. "James won't tell anybody, will he?"

I raised an eyebrow. For all she knew, I had some matter to discuss that pertained to our womanhood. Granted, I *wasn't* here to talk about that, but she didn't know that.

"It really is something I'd rather speak about alone."

"Fine, if you'd rather wait."

She didn't seem at all in a rush to finish.

Well, if that was the way she wanted it. It wasn't of immediate importance, anyway, but I *was* worried about Katherine. She had recovered from her initial post-battle shock enough to function again, but she hardly spoke to me—it was one-word answers or grunts—and when I asked her about it, she didn't even provide an excuse, just shrugged. Something was wrong with her, and I had to figure out how to fix it.

I had resigned myself to helping George write letters—I didn't consider myself especially proficient, but he hardly knew how to write his own name—and I'd been spelling out words for him for nearly an hour, dotted by an occasional hint from him that I should just write the whole letter for him. I was cooking up an explanation for how my father had not taught me how to plant seed by doing it for me when Beth marched up beside us.

"I'm ready to talk now. Where do you want to go?"

I was in the middle of spelling out the word "regiment"—probably incorrectly, due to my poor skills—so I hesitated.

"Why don't you sit—"

"If you can't say it in front of James, you obviously aren't willing to talk to anyone besides me about it, so where do you want to go?"

George mouthed, *"Who's James?"* I didn't want to explain it to him, so I shrugged.

"We'll be back before long," I told him.

Beth's arms were crossed, and she dropped them to her sides as I rose and led her out to the open field at the outskirts of the camp. There were a few men gambling nearby, and a few using homemade slingshots to shoot at birds in the trees. I had never seen such a thing before, not from someone older than twelve, and I was certain they would face trouble from their officers for acting like children, but I doubted they would be caught. We weren't far out from camp, but far enough that nobody cared much.

"What bothers you?" Beth asked, and I couldn't tell if she was upset with me or not.

She had seemed disturbed about my aversion to chatting with James, but she was now acting perfectly reasonable, so maybe she'd moved on from it.

"I'm worried about Katherine. She isn't speaking to me."

"Is she mad at you?"

"No, and she doesn't refuse to see me. She just doesn't talk."

Beth shrugged.

"Are you sure she's not just distancing herself from you?"

"Why would she do that?"

"She doesn't need you anymore."

Her words cut like ice, and I was about to lash out at her when she continued, "We brought her here and tried to help her, but now she's been a nurse for more than a week now. She's probably made friends with the other nurses. Maybe they've even offered to help feed her. She doesn't need a random, suspiciously sympathetic soldier hanging by her side anymore."

"I'm not suspiciously sympathetic!"

Her eyes widened. *Are you kidding me?*

"Thousands of soldiers passed by her that day, and hardly one of them even looked at her. They didn't care. So why would you?"

"I care because—"

"Save the explanation. *I* know why you care. She doesn't."

I didn't know what she thought she knew.

Was she referring to the fact that I was a woman, or did she think it was for some other reason?

"Okay, but after all we've done for her, wouldn't she continue to be thankful instead of ignoring us?"

"Does she not still accept our food?"

"Yes."

"And does she not show gratitude every time we give it to her?"

"She does."

"Then what more do you want from her? She doesn't need to be your friend. You brought her here, and you feed her. If she knew who you are, then of course you could try to mentor her. But she doesn't, so it's better for you to let someone else do it. There are plenty of nurses around her. If she needs help, she can go to them."

A pause resounded through the open field. A few birds squawked at the soldiers who were slingshotting. I tried to come to terms with what Beth was telling me.

"You've done your part, Caleb."

The word *Caleb* sounded harsh and unfriendly; she never called me that in private. Maybe she thought it was easier; if she never called me Cassie anymore, it would be hard for her to slip up when we were around the others.

Somehow, that didn't seem like the real explanation.

I breathed in the swirling, fresh breeze.

"I wish I could do more."

"Me, too."

I had questions for her. Mostly, questions like: *Why are you so close with James lately? Why are you worried about me being friends with Katherine if you spend all your time hanging around that negro? Aren't you worried what people think of you?* I didn't have the courage, though, and I knew she would be angry with me if I asked. She wouldn't give me answers.

I supposed, altogether, that there were worse things to worry about.

No matter how I tried to believe Beth—because what she'd said *had* made sense, after all—something struck me as wrong. Katherine wasn't just distancing herself from me. She was troubled. There was a deep, profound sadness in her, a haunted look in her eyes that had nothing to do with me. I didn't know what would happen if nobody helped her.

Yet it was as Beth had said.

She doesn't need you anymore.

I entered the hospital with a small sigh. Beth would frown at me for doing this, but I had done as she recommended for several days now—perhaps a week. I had left Katherine alone. Something was wrong with her, and I knew it. Except for her brief mealtime handouts, I didn't speak with her. She would come to us quickly, and I would pass her a handful of beans and meat—when there was any—and I longed to ask her if she was okay. It would be so simple: *"How are you, Katherine? Do you need anything?"* But I believed Beth. It wasn't my place.

Just this once, I had promised myself. I was only checking on her.

She wasn't here. There were two dozen patients at least and a quarter as many nurses, but not one of them was young Katherine.

"Can I help you with something?" the one named Jane asked politely.

"Where's Katherine?"

She raised an eyebrow at me, then looked around.

"We haven't seen her since last night. I suppose she's taking a break."

"A break? Does she do that often?"

"Never before."

"Did she simply disappear from her tent? Why isn't anyone looking for her?"

Her expression said, *"Are you joking?"*

"We are all very busy. She doesn't seem to be formally registered, so she can't be punished as a deserter, and we have no authority to search for her. It wouldn't be our job, anyway."

"Whose job is it, then?"

"Nobody's, as far as I know. I've never heard of the army searching after a missing nurse. They hardly go after soldiers, as I'm sure you know."

Our superiors sure made it sound like we'd be hunted like dogs if we deserted, but I'd heard from the other men that this wasn't quite the case. So, yes, I did know what she meant. Really, I didn't expect them to send out a search party for Katherine if they couldn't even give her food, but it was frustrating that she'd vanished, and nobody was even worried about her.

"Don't worry about her," Jane said. "I really don't think she's missing."

On the other hand, I really did.

Beth, when I told her my plans, was calm.

"The captain will never allow it."

"Did you think I was planning to tell him?"

She crossed her arms in her typical gesture.

"If you actually do it, *I* will tell him."

I sneered. "You wouldn't!"

Her expression did not falter.

"She's *missing*, Tim."

I used the name because we were in the middle of the camp. We had a leisurely day ahead of us, though tomorrow we would be marching again. All the more reason to locate Katherine as soon as possible.

"God knows what kind of trouble she can get herself into. I have to find her."

"Are you sure she's missing? Have you not looked for her here in the camp?"

"Of course I have! Nobody has seen her this morning. She's obviously run off somewhere, and I doubt it will take long to find her, since I know she wouldn't run far."

"How do you know that? If she left last night, she could be two towns away by now."

"On the day I found her, she was hardly a mile away from where she'd been that morning. She could have gone on to another town, but she didn't. I don't know why, believe me, but I don't think she would stray far from the camp this time, either. Maybe she *thinks* she wants to run away, but I don't believe she really does."

"*I* think you don't know her as well as you think you do."

"You think you know her better?"

"No! But you've hardly known her two weeks. You don't know what she's thinking. You don't know what she wants."

"I guessed pretty well the first time, I think."

I was talking about when I offered her food and a place to stay.

"I won't be gone more than a few hours. If she's not close like I think she is, then I suppose I'll have to admit that she's gone, and I can't find her. But if she's right under our noses, Tim, I need to find her."

She didn't look happy about it, but she conceded.

"Fine. What do you want from me, though?"

"Just don't tell anyone I'm gone."

It wouldn't be hard, really. I doubted anyone except perhaps George would ask after me, and Beth could make up an excuse.

Thus I went. A horse would have made things mighty easier, but there was no way for me to acquire one without explaining what I was doing. I didn't think I would have to go far, anyhow.

Even the nearest town, which was the farthest I could possibly imagine Katherine venturing into, was only a few miles out. The road there was my path because though I wasn't sure whether Katherine had gone that far, she probably would have taken this road. Whether it was because she wanted to reach the town or simply because it was better than wandering about the forest, I wasn't sure.

I had left camp as the midday sun settled in and vowed to return before sunset. Granted, that was more than "a few hours," but it wouldn't be a problem. If we'd had drills, as we had for the past few days, then I would be short for time, but everybody was busy preparing to march—packing up tents, loading the carts, and so on.

With each step of dust that I kicked up, swirled a thousand thoughts. Would I find that young girl on this lonely road? There were fears I dared not voice, nor even think, but they bubbled up like bile because I had nobody and nothing to distract me. Surely, nothing had happened to Katherine.

Finally, I reached town, and nothing. She had not been idling by the side of the road. She had not been hiding behind a tree, where she had jumped out to greet me before.

I didn't know what I had expected.

So, with a heavy heart and a stirring feeling that I should be getting back soon, I entered the town of Knoxville.

It was a run-down little village. There wasn't even a post office; the whole town was little more than a cluster of houses and a butcher's shop. Lush trees and grassy fields stretched out on all sides, giving it a rather quaint feel, except for this: there was nobody here.

I was not surprised to find the town abandoned; most places in our path were quickly being deserted. It was a chilling sight, though; this place was full of ghosts. I ducked into the first house I saw, just to look. If not for the missing rifle from the rifle hook and the resounding hollowness, it could have still been occupied, by the looks of it. A small pile of logs sat by the fireplace, and a large pot with a dirty wooden spoon on the other side. If I were to venture upstairs, I would probably find the blankets still on the beds, though I was sure the valuables were gone.

On to the next house. I didn't know why I was even doing this. I wasn't going to find anything.

As soon as I creaked the door open, I heard a loud rustle. I whipped around, wishing I'd brought my rifle or a bayonet at least.

A sniff. "Caleb?"

I squinted.

"Katherine? Oh, God, I've been looking for you!" I stepped toward her, resisting the urge to embrace her. "What happened to you? Why did you leave?"

She shook her head, her body shrinking from me.

"It's nothing."

"How long have you been here?"

Since dawn."

"You traveled all this way in the middle of the night? Do you have any idea what could have happened to you?"

Her back was turned to me.

"Do you want some water? I found a well just outside, so I brought some in. I don't see any cups, though…"

"Katherine," I said. "You must tell me immediately what is going on."

She spun and crossed her arms.

"I don't want to talk right now. Okay? I don't belong with the army, especially not yours. I belong here."

"Alone?"

"I'm going to move on, of course. I don't intend to stay here more than a few days. Just long enough to see what's here to take."

"This is absurd." I bit my lip. "It's absurd. You were safe with us! You had food, shelter, and a *duty*. How could you abandon that?"

"It wasn't much of a duty, was it, if you were the only one who came looking for me?"

"Did you expect a whole company to come after you? That's not how it works."

"I don't care how it works! I can't work for you people, and that's the end of it!"

"I'm not leaving until you come with me."

"Well, I suppose you'll be staying a long time, then." With her chin lifted, she moved gracefully toward the counter. "Are you sure you don't want water?"

Refusing to answer, I stared out the cobwebbed window. For all her apparent attempts to appear otherwise, she still looked ragged and lost: her dress sleeves had fallen haphazardly off her shoulders, her hair looked like a bird's nest of tangles and knots, and dirt dotted her cheeks. She was different, and yet so similar to how I had found her: desperate, hungry, alone. There was no way I was letting her end up like that again.

The wind fluttered outside the open window. I took a deep breath.

"Sometimes I wish I were dead."

Her head jerked toward me—a good sign.

"I've been through much in this war. I've bled and starved and lost, just like you. So no matter how bad you're feeling now, with God as my witness, I've felt it, too."

"I don't know—"

"I haven't a clue why you left. You don't need to tell me if you don't want to, but I need you to believe me when I say that no matter how bad it gets back at the camp, the rest of the world can be much, much worse. You don't need me to tell you that, though, do you?"

She'd lost her home and her family at the very least. And though I'd so hoped otherwise, it turned out that my finding her didn't solve much at all.

"I suppose I can't force you to come back, but I want you to know that whatever is troubling you, I can help. I *will* help."

She shook her head.

"You can't help me. You have no idea what's been done to me, and *you* were one of the people that did it."

"You've lost the most important people in your whole life?"

Slowly, almost mutinously, she nodded.

"Me, too."

She was silent.

The afternoon stretched out, endless like the sunshine and cornfields of the days many years ago, before this. I wondered if she was remembering, too—if she wished she could go back to simpler times.

As the sky began to crack into myriad colors, I stood from my rickety, painful chair.

"I have to get back," I said. "Now's your last chance to come with me."

Without waiting for a response, I set out. The seeds of panic began to set in—what if Beth had ratted on me? What if somebody noticed I was missing? They were unfounded, though, and I knew it, but in the deep part of the heart where anxiety upsets all rationality, I was starting to grow anxious.

It was then that I heard the footsteps. Just like the first time.

Chapter Fifteen

Beth's attitude upon my return had appeared to settle between grudging respect and snobbish disapproval, both of which I was more used to dealing out than receiving. I accepted it though, at least because I understood it. It was how I'd felt about Joshua, about Beth, now about Katherine. It was a motherly trait, perhaps; that's how it seemed in Beth, at least, though she was only a few years elder to me.

So I was surprised to see her sneak into the parlor of an abandoned little home close to camp. She was not the only one, by any means—too many soldiers to count had felt their fingers grow sticky and seized the opportunity to do a little scavenging. The captains were very strictly against it, but that didn't seem to stop anyone. It was mostly the younger ones who broke the rule. The veterans turned up their noses and smoked tobacco while the camp emptied out.

I had intended to stay with them, but when I saw Beth slip away, I couldn't help but trot behind her. As soon as she closed the little house's door behind her, I slipped into sight from behind a nearby tree and quietly followed her steps.

"General Order Number Twenty-Six," I quoted upon entering. "Any soldier or army follower who shall be convicted of a crime of arson or robbery or who shall be caught pillaging shall be shot, and officers and non-commissioners ditto have the right to shoot pillagers in the act."

Beth, who had been searching the bedroom, snorted at the oft-repeated but rarely-enforced law.

"Don't be smart with me."

"It's an official order," I said. "I never thought you one to break the rules, especially when 'officers and non-commissioners ditto have the right to—'"

"Enough," she said harshly, but her eyes glittered with

amusement.

"We could be shot just for being here."

"I hope to be shot for a bit more," she said, pulling a ruby ring from her pocket just long enough for me to see how valuable it was.

"Impressive," I drawled, eyes wide in shock. "Enough to feed us for months. Greed finally got the best of you, Beth?"

"I would call it 'survival.'"

Her expression turned distant for a fleeting moment. She pulled the ring out again and rubbed it between her fingers.

"If we survive, where will we go? We have no money and no home to go back to."

"God will lead the way, I'm sure of it."

"Oh, the same way he's led us so smoothly thus far?"

I didn't have an answer for that.

"Did you find anything else?" I asked, after a pause.

She shook her head. "But I only checked the one bedroom. There must be another place."

"As I hear it, the slaves are saying that much has been buried in the backyards."

Not all of the citizens in this particular town had fled, but even the ones who had fled had left their negroes to rot here. I doubt that they made a show of indicating to the slaves where they'd hidden their loot, but most seemed to know. Apparently, the ones who had fled had done so in the hope that they'd be able to return and dig up their goods (and they hadn't just buried them to make sure we never touched them), and somehow they believed that the slaves they'd abandoned were still loyal enough not to spill their secrets. Their foolishness was our luck.

She glanced out the window. The grasses outside were much too wide for us to just grab some tools and start digging. We'd be here for weeks.

"If only we had an idea where to start."

We traipsed back into camp, somber but a little giddy with our newfound treasure. It was a simple little thing—the ring, but at the camp, we had endured days without food, cold nights without enough blankets, and, worse, we had watched our comrades rot away in the hospital without the power to help make them well. A ring worth a month's salary? That, at least, was something to smile about.

Katherine appeared from nowhere.

"You missed dinner," she said.

At first I wasn't bothered by it because although most men tended to eat around sundown, pulling out pots and pans and cooking mysterious concoctions with bacon grease, it wasn't as if there was a penalty for saving one's food for later.

Then I remembered. That meant Katherine hadn't eaten, either. I knew she would be fine—Beth and I would probably pull out our food as soon as we sat down—but a sharp jab of guilt stirred in my stomach. Waiting a few hours for dinner was not so bad, but watching everyone else munch merrily away and wondering if she would get to eat at all tonight must have been quite uncomfortable. I had experienced the same, and it was quite awful at times.

Ah, but Katherine would have to warm herself to it. If this was hard for her, winter would be brutal. Still, when I pulled out the hardtack and beans and softened it in a cup of tepid coffee, I made sure to give her a little more than usual.

As soon as Beth had wolfed down her food, she disappeared. I determined initially not to wonder about her—how much trouble could she stir up in camp, anyhow? But as it turned out, I didn't have to.

Not twenty feet away, there she was with the thick, dark man she called her friend. Beth and James were sitting with their foreheads almost touching—in a position that could have been shrugged off as a friendly conversation, but to me it was disturbingly intimate.

"What are you looking at?"

Katherine's voice had startled me from my contemplation. I gulped the last mouthful of beans.

"Nothing. Nothing, I was just distracted."

"Well, what distracted you?"

I chuckled.

"There are some things you don't need to know."

She frowned, apparently dissatisfied with that answer. I would have been, too, if I were her. It was funny to me, observing the immaturity in her sometimes. I was hardly more than a year older than her, yet sometimes it felt as if we were decades apart. Whether that was my fault or hers, I didn't know.

I was accustomed to Katherine's quietness, but when several minutes passed without a single word from her, I began to grow twitchy. Perhaps it was my turn to say something? I couldn't remember.

"How is everything in the hospital?" I asked, stuttering a bit.

"Good." Then she was still.

"Does it bother you?"

"Does what bother me?"

"Uh, I don't know…you seemed a little squeamish at first, that's all."

"I was never squeamish," she insisted, though it was really undeniable.

For God's sake, after one day of battle, she had nearly turned green.

"I don't think things have gotten better, but I've learned to cope with it, I suppose. How would I survive if I fainted at the sight of blood?"

She chuckled, as if it were a joke, but considering this was the very question I had been asking myself when first I saw her in the hospital, it didn't seem so funny to me.

A peal of raucous laughter. It was George and Martin, a few

seats away from us. Both of them were having a wild discussion that put mischievous grins on both their faces, and I felt a pang of jealousy. That childishness, that sense of fun—I looked down upon it sometimes, but in others, I yearned for it. How nice it would be to have some *fun*.

I spotted a group of gambling men, and I recognized their game immediately. I was a little hesitant because it would be improper for Katherine to participate in such a thing, but none of the men would care if she watched. I tapped her arm and smiled.

"Have you ever heard of Faro?" I asked.

It was George's idea, and he dragged Beth and me along—as well as four others—unaware of the uncomfortable tacitness between us. It wasn't as if we didn't speak because we hated each other (or, at least, I didn't hate Beth), but we never launched into a friendly conversation as we had done so easily before. Because neither of us knew any of the other men well besides George, who was traipsing at the head of our pack through the forest, we inevitably found ourselves side-by-side, silent companions on the journey.

"What exactly are we doing here?" One of the men nudged him. "Are you hoping to find Judies in a town like this?"

My palms immediately began to sweat. I was about to head to the hills on some dry excuse, dragging Beth along behind me, when George snorted and said, "No! We're going to see if any of the ladies here have anything for us."

I assumed he meant food or bed because he certainly wouldn't be knocking on doors asking widows to hand over their valuables—I was sure he wasn't that sort—but still, it was strange. However, the officers had never prohibited us from accepting hospitality, and as long as we were in camp in the morning and as long as we didn't cause a ruckus in town, they wouldn't spare a thought on where we'd slept or eaten.

"There's an idea." His companion chuckled. "If we see any cattle around, I'll pull out my bayonet." He glanced down at his waist. "Shame I didn't bring my gun."

"We're not stealing livestock," George said firmly. "We're going to play nice."

I got the sense that the words "playing nice" weren't familiar to the rest of these men.

Beth stumbled over something.

"Hey!" she cried. "I found something!"

It was a small wooden box. Inside, as we discovered, were two pearl bracelets and a number of tintype portraits. The bracelets seemed valuable, but otherwise, the whole box was of little worth to anyone but its owner—why would they leave it out here?

"Whose is it?" someone demanded.

"Well, how are we supposed to know?" George retorted.

I pointed through the trees at a small cottage.

"I would guess they live there."

Although in plain sight, it was a few minutes' walk, so we grabbed the box and strolled over. If there was someone there still, they must be having a real fright seeing seven soldiers march up to their home at once, but she would soon know that we meant no harm. At least, we hoped.

The back door swung open, startling us.

"Come here with that, you monsters! You have no right to steal my belongings!"

Beth was the one holding it.

"We don't mean to steal it, madam, only to give it back."

The woman stepped backward and frowned at us.

"You aren't here to rob me?" she asked accusingly.

We all glanced at each other.

"We've never done such a thing to a soul before," George volunteered. "Unless you'd like us to start with you."

He was joking, but a hint of fear glinted in her eyes.

Beth approached her with the box.

"Here, take it."

Her eyes started to shine as if wet as she took the box back.

"Well, come in then, all of you. I'll get you something to drink."

George didn't even turn back to us and give a cue; he just stepped right through the door behind her, and we all followed like a line of ants.

The place was old and lonely in a way that made my heart ache with pity. It was a single story, so the bedrooms must all have been spread on the ground floor, but we could only see the parlor room and the kitchen. The furniture was not cobwebbed, but it looked as if everything was just shy of it—like we could come back tomorrow, and every chair and table would be covered with them. However, a sofa was indeed a sofa, and we weren't about to check it for maggots when we'd all been sitting on twigs and dead leaves since we could remember—that was how it was in the camp.

The lady emerged from her little kitchen with a wooden pitcher and a few cups—not enough for all of us, but we would share. We gratefully poured lemonade and swallowed it like we'd never tasted such a delight before, and it did so feel like it. It was one of those instances where dormant thirst creeps up on one when they taste the first sweet sip of something and realize how well and truly they have been craving it.

I had a thousand and one questions for this desperate but dignified lady. She must have been in her fifties, so perhaps she had sons in the war? They would have been Rebels, so it felt improper to ask, but I wondered. And why had she dropped her valuables off in the middle of the forest, not even burying them, instead of keeping them close to her until the last minute?

It seemed as if there were some questions on her mind, too, but she sat with us as we gulped down our lemonade like children. She was seemingly unaffected by having seven enemy soldiers in her sitting room, especially after her initial panic.

George broke the silence.

"I'm George, by the way. And this is Carter, Walker, John, Tim, Caleb, and Ron." He gestured to each of us as he said our names.

Our hostess nodded.

"I'm Sally."

It seemed such a young name for a woman of her age.

Before the silence could last too long, George began, "The rumors about us must have been pretty bad if you hid all your belongings like that, am I correct?"

She bit her lip. Her eyes were small and tilted down on the outsides just enough to give her a permanent sad, thoughtful look.

"Ah, you're right. The dailies had us all thinking you would come right in and burn our houses down. I figured I would have time enough to slip out the back door, but I wanted to make sure that box was safe. But you boys would never do such an awful thing, would you? You seem so friendly."

We glanced at each other, thinking of all the houses we'd burned already.

"No," George replied. "We would never."

The sun was starting to sink beneath the trees, only an hour or so before we'd have to leave.

Through the window, a bird cawed loudly, a sharp sound that tingled my ears. Sally laughed.

"Those are the crows. We get at least two or three each morning, and they start even before dawn. My boys used to go out there and throw rocks to get them to be quiet, but it never quite worked."

She chuckled.

"Now I like the sound."

Walker, an Irish boy whose accent was sometimes too thick to understand, nodded.

"At home we used to get them, too. I used to slingshot them and actually hit a few."

"Poor birds," she said quietly. "But it must have been your youth that drove you to such cruelty."

Suddenly, without explanation, I was filled with sizzling anger.

"I have seen more cruelties by grown men than by boys. Wouldn't you agree, Tim?"

Beth elbowed me.

"I don't know what you mean," she replied with discomfort.

"Are your sons Rebels, Miss Sally?"

She flinched.

"Yes. They've been gone two years."

"Then why are you letting us in your home? They could kill us tomorrow, or we could kill them. We might burn down your house come morning. So why do you let us in as guests?"

Beth gritted her teeth.

"I don't know why you speak such nonsense," she hissed, yet somehow it managed to sound polite.

George interjected, "He doesn't mean it, madam. He's been a bit moody lately." He shot a threatening glance at me.

"I just don't understand," I seethed, "why we're pretending like we're friends. I lost a brother to men like your sons, and if your sons were the ones who did it, I'd take my bayonet to them, Miss Sally, without a thought. If your sons are the ones who made me lose him, then I will make sure you suffer as I have."

My face was hot, and I couldn't believe I'd just said those words. Was this real?

Sally looked as if she was about to faint.

"I thought," she whispered, her lip trembling. "I thought you weren't so different from my boys. But you aren't like them at all."

A tiny tear trickled from her eye.

"Well, I'm sorry, Miss Sally," I said. "Have your pearls and photographs back, but I'm not going to sit here and drink lemonade with a traitor."

To the tune of George cursing under his breath and the rest of the men trying to reassure Sally, I stormed out of the house. I didn't care if I had to sleep on the ground tonight with no blanket.

The truth was I didn't know what had sparked my burst of rage. I felt some degree of remorse for poor Miss Sally, but I didn't regret what I had said. I hoped I hadn't made her faint, but given the chance, I would say that same thing again. Something about the sweet smell of lemonade and lavender reminded me of home, a place I could never go back to. I could never go back without Joshua.

Before I reached camp, I stopped by a tree and slid down against the trunk until I was sitting on the ground. In a surprisingly short amount of time, Beth came stomping into the field, and she walked a few circles before she noticed me. Her face was a picture of pure rage. She knelt down by me, looked me straight in the eyes with her lips shaking in anger, and slapped me.

It hurt less than last time, maybe because I didn't care so much about the pain.

"I cannot believe you," she said. "I can't believe what you did to that poor woman. She was about to offer us a place to sleep, and if George and the others got sent off because of you, things are not going to be easy for us here in the camp."

"Why didn't you just stay with them?" I demanded. "If I made such a mess of things."

"I don't know," she said. "I wish I had."

"Then go," I said. "I'll recover."

She sat down beside me and was quiet for a long time.

"I don't think so," she said.

"I will recover. I'm not going any—"

"Not that. I'm not going to leave you. That's what I meant."

I didn't respond. The sun was dipping beneath the earth, and the sky was caught in that tender moment just before everything goes dark. We'd have to get back if we wanted to set up our sleeping bags, but I didn't want to move. We could stay here all night, Beth and I, touching shoulders and pretending everything was all right.

"You do realize," she asked, "how absolutely childish and inappropriate you were?"

"Of course I do."

Beth sighed deeply, the kind that sinks down to the heart and means, *I don't even know what to say about this*.

"I want him back, Beth. Every single minute of every day. I want him back."

"Me, too," she said.

A long pause.

"Me, too."

Chapter Sixteen

Our camp was close to the road mainly because there was no point in straying too far when we would be getting right back on it soon anyhow. We often saw stragglers pass by, usually rugged farmer folk, but occasionally, there was a family of well-dressed people who scowled as if the idea of walking on a dirt road—well, I was sure it was the idea of fleeing, really—was beneath them.

Today, I happened to be walking about near the dusty path when a small negro girl shuffled by. She was obviously a freed slave, or a runaway—the President had declared all slaves to be free (it was in one of the dailies a year ago, and some men had a fit about it), but that meant nothing to any traitor. They thought they had their own President, so they didn't listen to the real one.

No matter what the story, I was certain I was looking at an orphan. Even if her parents were still alive, I'd heard enough from the negroes who still populated the camp to guess that she was separated from whatever family she may have had. Mother, father, sisters, brothers—if they were alive, she wouldn't know where they were.

However, I shouldn't have thought of such things. No matter how unfortunate her life may have been, I had felt for enough people already. Sympathy was a womanly weakness that I should've shorn with the clothes of my gender. I was not so vulnerable now.

She came closer until I was almost in her sight, and I considered moving away to avoid the hassle of exchanging pleasantries—which, in this case, would be a little more than nodding coldly at her, if anything at all. Too late for any of that, though—she had already seen me, and she regarded me with a meek curiosity that I supposed was typical for her kind.

It was after several seconds of her staring that I asked, "Do you need something?" in a gruff, harsh tone that I was actually rather proud of.

She shook her head as if she wished to say more but couldn't. I wondered what town she'd come from and if her mistress had fled already and left her with nothing to do but flee herself. And then I remembered what the other men had been saying about how the slaves often knew where the valuables were hidden. Suddenly, I had an idea.

"Do you have a master?" I asked, uncertain how proper the question would be.

"He sent me on an errand," the girl said quickly, fearfully.

I could tell it was a lie.

"Because if you don't, that's all right," I assured. "I only thought that if your master had set you free before leaving his home, you might be able to help the army."

"My master sent me on an errand," she repeated. "He told me I shouldn't talk to anyone."

"We can help you," I lied. "I'll protect you."

She stopped.

"What are you asking of me?"

"Do you know of any place where your master may have hidden his valuables?" I asked. "Maybe he buried them somewhere?"

"I really can't tell you that," she said, her eyes downturned. "Master Hughes would never allow it."

"He'll never know," I said. "If you just show me where he hid the items, I won't ever tell him a word, and you'll be freed for your service to the Union."

Of course, she was already free, really, but she didn't seem to know that.

The girl looked about nervously as if deciding whether to run.

"Your master isn't home, am I right?"

She nodded.

"He left for a few days and sent me to run some errands. I can't go back without doing them."

"Where did he send you?"

Her hands were trembling.

"To the next town over. Named Chesterfield. Please, sir, if you'll let me be on my way, I must get back."

"There is no next town over, girl. Everyone is gone. We've taken Chesterfield. So you'll have to turn back because there's nothing for you."

I had sensed untruth in her story. Why would her master leave his slave—or slaves—alone at the estate if he was gone? Wouldn't he be afraid of them escaping as I guessed this girl was doing now? Were the slaves really so obedient? I doubted it, especially because the master must have known how close our army was. Why would he leave the slaves alone when we, who would free them, were so near? Maybe he trusted them extremely well. What did I know about the peculiar institution, after all? I guessed, though, that this girl had run away somehow, and she didn't trust me enough to tell me.

If her master had indeed buried his valuables in the back of the woods as Miss Sally had, it would be easy for this girl to show me where it was so we could quickly dig it up and be gone. She could then come back to camp with us and live with the other negroes. It would be simple and easy, and if I came back with something of value, Beth would be greatly pleased with me.

So I did convince her after a few minutes, and she led the way back to her master's house. Was she hungry for the freedom I offered? Probably. Was she afraid of me? Surely, at least a little. But things would be all right.

When I asked, she told me her name was Constance. I felt no sympathy for this girl, but I could know her name.

Constance led me between two trees with their branches stretched out as if to touch one another, as if they were old friends saying hello.

"It is here," she said, and we dipped our fingers into the soft earth. I would have brought a shovel, but she told me it was shallow enough.

I would have told someone, but nobody cared. I was not a deserter if I was back for the morning march.

In the distance was the little farmhouse where her master must have lived. It was visible from where we were, just a shape against the lush landscape beyond but close enough to make out the door, the windows, and a little yard. Constance glanced back there every so often, and I followed her gaze. The house never changed, no matter how many times we looked.

"Were you the only slave?" I wanted to ask her. *"Did you ever know your mother or father? Did your master treat you well?"*

I did not ask any of these things, though, because she was a quiet girl, and I did not feel sympathy for her.

She helped me pull the box out. Three silver spoons and a few china teacups. They would be more difficult to slip into my coat to carry back, but it could be done.

I placed my hand on Constance's shoulder and was about to thank her when a booming voice interrupted us.

"What is this?"

It was the voice of a giant, a god. A monster.

"Constance," I whispered. "Run."

Before she could take two steps, he grabbed her.

"Not so fast," he hissed. "You're going to tell me exactly what you've been doing."

"You were gone," she said, her voice trembling. "You weren't supposed to come back."

"Things changed," he sneered.

He was formidable.

"And you," he said, turning to me. "What is your business? Should I report you for thievery?"

If anyone else had said it, I would have laughed; instead, I shivered. Yet I stood up taller and lifted my chin because I was a man, for now.

"I merely stumbled across this in the woods, sir. Is it theft if it's not on your property?"

It was a weak argument, but it was all I had.

"Not the spoons. The girl. Are you trying to take her from me?"

"As I see it, you abandoned her. So it looks like she was free for the taking."

"Well, that's not how I see it. So why don't you get your Yankee ass off my property before I give you a real lickin'."

"Constance doesn't belong to you!" I said. "Under United States law, she is free."

"You think I listen to your dumb Yankee laws? No, you'll have to pry her from my cold, dead hands," he promised, and I believed every word. He started to tug her away, and her eyes were filling with tears.

"Come on, you little bitch, I need to teach you a lesson."

"No!" I shouted. "You can't!"

I started to run after him, this menacing giant of a man and Constance with her silent screams. But there was no way to win. I could not out-wrestle this man.

"I'll come back for you," I shouted. "Constance, I'll come back!"

I couldn't tell if she heard me; if she did, she knew it was a lie. We would be leaving soon—what could I even do for her? I looked back at the dug-up treasure: the three spoons, the two teacups. The bastard hadn't even bothered to take them back; he was too angry at Constance. Or maybe, he thought he'd frightened me into leaving them alone. I picked them up and shoved them in my coat. This couldn't all have been for nothing.

From the house, I heard an angry masculine shout, and then screaming.

The Springfield rifle felt like a beast in the hands. When the battle for Rome, Georgia, erupted, I marched into the grassy field in awe of how it felt to hold it again. It had been so long since we had felt this great stirring.

The grass was long, lush, and crisp. We marched toward the Rebel line with great dignity—left, right, left, right as we had drilled since the beginning of time. When we crashed through their numbers and the bullets really began to fly, it felt like we were beginning anew.

Nobody ever spoke of war in the camp. Before I knew much about it, I had assumed that this was because it was so awful, and maybe for some it was, but for me it was something different. How could I explain how this felt? How could I comprehend how something so evil and terrible felt so good? God must have been thinking so little of me now.

The man in front of me fell with the roar of a lion. I stepped lithely over him, mouthing a silent prayer as I reloaded my gun and raised it to the Rebels.

I aimed square for the heart of the first man in gray who caught my eye. The bullet dove into his arm. I wondered if he would fall. Even if the wounds weren't great, I knew how some men chose to fall on their faces as soon as a bit of blood began to pool in their arms; they lay prostrate like corpses. Nobody would bother to shoot a dead man, they thought, but one could always tell the difference. I took special pleasure in dealing with these cowards.

We had been singing a song as we marched in, as we always did, but by now it had dissolved into a few broken chants by those who seemed to think that whistling a cheery little tune would keep God on their side. To my right, someone was humming—it must have been "Rally Round the Flag," but who but God could say for sure. He fell after a few minutes—it wasn't even a blow to the heart, though, and as I stepped around him, I was tempted to kick him. Not too hard, just enough to remind him of his weakness. There were worse wounds than his, and though he probably thought there was no chance that he would continue to march on, I knew differently.

He was only one man, though. The rest of us were strong. It was the Rebels who fell to their knees at the first sign of a bullet.

Deep into the Rebel lines, someone fell to his knees just in front of me, and as he craned his neck toward the sky, I caught a glimpse of his face. He had the messy hair and hopeful eyes of my brother, and for a moment I would have sworn I was glimpsing him in the flesh.

But this was not Joshua. This was one of the men who had taken him from me.

"Help!" he cried, though he knew that I was in blue, and he was in gray.

I stepped over him, not responding, but I was hit with a sudden ache of realization: he was someone's Joshua.

Well, if I had to lose mine, someone else could lose theirs, too.

The nurses were on the sidelines, helping the injured men stumble toward the hospital, and as a few of them started to shout for some matter or another, I turned my eye toward them. In that short second, I swore I saw the body of Beth's friend, James, on a stretcher.

Beth would be devastated. After the battle, when there was time to process all of this, we would have to visit the hospital together, and I would squeeze her shoulder sympathetically as she tried not to cry. If it was truly James, that is. But there were few enough negroes here now, so it wasn't hard to tell them apart.

So the bullets flew for hours, and many men lost a limb, and I managed to fight my way through it by biting my lip near to raw and firing enthusiastically with my almost-decent aim. Perhaps a better man than I had fallen—many probably had—but by some unseen grace or some unspoken curse, God had held my hand and marched with me through that battle in a way that he never did for Joshua or Nick or any of the hundreds of men whom I'd stepped over as I pushed on in the fight.

Eventually, we licked the Rebels.

When the end of the battle came, and we left that once-green field to soak up the blood, it did turn out to be James on that stretcher.

I had made my way to the hospital to check on the situation, and I found Beth standing over him with an expression that I understood quite intimately—an expression only shared between the two of us: a struggle between the necessity of staying strong and keeping a bold, masculine face and the desire to give in to womanly weeping.

He looked, quite frankly, dead. But if he was in the hospital, he couldn't be gone just yet. I knew Beth was holding onto this hope. Yet how could she look at that wide gash across his chest, hear his faint breathing, and honestly think there was a chance for him? Perhaps there was a chance—a slim, slim chance—but I didn't do chances anymore. I knew the odds.

There wasn't even a nurse around here. They were all running around, worked thin, the way I had been during my hospital days; there weren't enough of them to go around. I was tempted to say a word about it: *If only there were someone here to help him.* That wouldn't have improved matters.

Beth was strung tighter than a fiddle string.

"Where's Katherine? She must be around here. She can help us."

I shook my head.

"You don't want to do that to her. She's probably overworked as it is, and there's no way we could find her in a place this big."

The hospital spanned three tents, and even if we were to run back and forth in search of her, it was no use. I could not imagine if someone had tried to pull me away from my patients in order to give them special help. And there was the part I didn't want to say aloud: nobody, even a sweet girl like Katherine, would do that for a negro. Beth probably knew that, though.

"Well? What are we supposed to do? He needs help, Caleb. Why is nobody helping him?"

Surely, she *did* know why.

I shook my head.

"I'm sorry, Tim. I don't know. We just have to pray for him."

"No! We have to do more than that." Beth raised her eyebrows, and I didn't know what she was thinking, but I knew I didn't want to hear it. "We can do it."

"*We*?"

"Oh, Caleb, you know that we can help as well as any of these nurses. There's no point in waiting for one of them to come around."

"And what are we supposed to tell them?"

"We can make something up. It shouldn't be too difficult."

Her voice was unhinged, roughed out by an edge of desperation that made me want to flee.

Inevitably, it was I who did most of the work, allowing Beth to remain by James's side. As soon as I spotted the supply station, I left an anxious Beth to wait behind. Just as I had thought, one of the nurses raised a frazzled eyebrow at me.

"I'm helping," I said.

"Do you have any idea what you're doing?"

"I was a nurse for a while before they brought all you women in."

It seemed true enough. I'd heard there had actually been very few female nurses in the beginning, before they knew this would be a real war and not just a little spark of rebellion. (I'd heard a soldier or two speak around the campfire of his nursing days, but it was one of those things, like battle, that was hardly ever spoken of.) So it was a perfectly plausible story.

She squinted a bit at me. I knew she wasn't keen to believe me, but instead of interrogating me more, she said, "Well, if you're smart about it, you can help whomever you please. But if you make our job harder for us, you'll sure as God above hear from your captain about it," and was gone.

I came back with some bandage, and Beth hailed me like a hero.

"Don't thank me just yet," I reminded her and set to work.

It really did take a doctor to do this job. What was I supposed to do with this? I had grabbed the gauze thinking I could simply try to improve upon the hastily-applied bandages that were already wrapped around his chest, but that would not be enough. I could try to stitch the wound together, but for all I knew, there was still a bullet lodged in his chest. What if that just complicated things further? But there was no way he would survive with such an open, bleeding wound.

"Tim," I instructed, putting pressure on the bleeding, "go back there and get a needle and thread."

She trotted eagerly over and came back in seconds with the material. Thankfully, James was unconscious—the pain of stitches was nothing compared to the pain of an amputation, but it was still better that he didn't feel it.

And thus I set to work. I had done a fair share of stitches in my time, but I still wasn't entirely comfortable. I preferred cotton and linens, to be sure. Human skin wasn't an ideal material for this kind of work. Still, I finished it with some amount of pride in my labor. If anything was going to help him live, this would be it.

"What do we do now?" Beth asked.

"We wait and call a doctor when we can."

I didn't tell her how risky it still was, that there was probably a bullet lodged in his chest and by sewing over it, I may have really screwed things up. I didn't say that I was only guessing at solutions here.

Her eyes were watery, and she pursed her lips as if trying to hold it in.

"Thank you."

I shrugged it off with an, "It was no problem," hoping that my masculine tone would remind her where we were.

We weren't the only soldiers helping in the hospital. In my nursing days, we certainly had many who traipsed in after battle, and if they were still able, they would eagerly accept instructions from us. It wasn't hard for them, really, if they were told what to do: "Keep pressing down on the wound with your hand until I come back," or, "Give him a bit of whiskey and see if that helps the pain." Thus it was with the dozen or so other men in the tent with us. In the commotion of the hospital setting, I could see them helpfully carting materials around to the nurses and even holding down legs for amputations—though I'd only seen one or two today so far. Usually, those didn't start to pick up for about a day; it was hard to tell before then whether there was a risk of gangrene. Once I actually realized how many soldiers were here, it dawned on me why nobody was suspicious of us. We were just like everybody else.

And that was probably why a nurse scurried to my side suddenly and dropped a bloody towel into my hands.

"I need you to help that Irishman over there. Check if he's still bleeding and put pressure on the wound. If he's not, help the ones around him. Thank you, kind sir. And you can take your fellow with you if you like." She nodded toward Beth, who was standing behind me with a slight air of childish shyness.

"Well," I said. "I suppose we should go, then."

Beth looked extremely reluctant.

"Come, it'll be fine. We'll be close, so we can see when he wakes up. Then you can go back."

She shrugged, but I knew the words she wasn't saying: *I want to stay with him.* Still, she knew as well as I that there was work for us to do.

The Irishman, whom we spotted easily by the light hair and freckles, was conscious, and when we approached him, he started to babble in a heavy accent.

"Oh, bless your heart! Where did you come from? Oh, that nurse sent you, didn't she? I should have been watching, but I was distracted. How foolish is this? I'd better not die from something like this, let me say, because this was a quite stupid one. I saw the bullet come right toward me, and I was about to duck when my brain just froze—you know? I have no idea how it happened, and by God, I hope it doesn't again, because this is not good, not good at all. The point is, I could have missed this one, but I didn't. I suppose I'll just have more scars to show for it now. You got any scars?"

I was busy putting pressure on his wound, which was near the rib cage, and I'd blocked out his stream of words, so I didn't realize he had asked me a question until I paid attention to the silence around us. Beth was working with the man next to us, and she kept gesturing to me, wide-eyed and clueless, to give her instruction. It was hard to pay attention to her when this boy was peppering me with a restated version of whatever he was trying to ask me.

"Just press as hard as you can," I told her. "You'll have to do it for a long time." I turned back to the Irish boy. "I'm sorry, I didn't hear you just then. What did you say?"

"I asked if you had any scars."

"Oh."

I actually had to think about that one. I'd had some scrapes, as many as the next man, but I hadn't sustained a real injury yet, not that I'd had to be hospitalized for. Had a few bullets grazed my ears and my elbows? Sure, but none had dug into the skin. Now that I thought about it, I was extremely lucky. It was only a matter of time before I got a shell in my forearm.

"No, I haven't."

"Not a single one?"

"Well, I haven't been in the service very long. I only joined just before the march, and I suppose we haven't seen as much battle on this march as you folks are used to."

"Yes, well, that's unfortunate for you. Because what's the point of it all if we don't get to shoot a few Rebels, eh?"

I was inclined to agree. It was surprising, though, that he agreed with me. I hadn't reached a consensus about what most of the men believed about this whole war; for as many who were ready to strap on their boots and start firing at the first sign of a Rebel, there was a number who thought this whole thing was a fool's game. Mostly, the veterans thought so, which was a shame. They were usually the ones who acted with a levelheaded bravery, not the cowardice or downright stupidity in some of us younger ones.

"I suppose it is a shame. I won't complain about not having been shot, but I would hate to return home without a few scars to show for it." It was nice, I thought, to pretend that I had a home to return to.

"You got a wife back where you're from?"

"No."

It was an awkward response; I felt that I had left something hanging.

"Not yet, at least."

Truly, I hadn't thought of this. Would I take a husband when I returned and how? What man would take a soldier for his wife? I could lie about where I'd been, but something about that didn't sit right with me. It would be difficult to be dishonest about such a monumental thing. Although it wouldn't be hard to just pretend I'd been a nurse this whole time, it was the sentiment that made the difference—being a soldier had changed me somehow.

"Ah, that's a shame. It's good to have someone to write home to, you know? It reminds one that he won't be here forever."

"I actually like it here," I thought. *"I don't know if I'll ever want to leave."*

Where would I go? Back to Illinois? I had nobody there. And would Beth want me to come back with her? It was not as if I could ask that of her, though she might offer. One might imagine that it would be freedom to not have a home: I could go anywhere. I could hightail it to New York or Chicago, one of the booming cities out West. I could save up some money and purchase a plot of land in one of the western territories, where things were quiet and people were few. I could be married, or I could be alone for the rest of my life.

Somehow, these things didn't encourage me.

"Yes," I told the Irish boy, finally. "It is a shame that I do not have a wife."

After another quarter-hour of conversation, while I treated the boy's wounds, Beth tapped my shoulder.

"He is waking," she whispered.

I wasn't in a hurry to heed her. He could be fully awake, but he might have shifted a mere quarter-inch, and she would have said the same. However, when I finally extracted myself away from the boy to look, it seemed that he was beginning to wake.

"I think you're okay now," I told the Irish boy. "I'm going to bandage you, and then I'm going to let you rest. If you need anything, I'll be near. My name is Caleb."

He nodded pleasantly as I did the bandaging, and when it was done, I slipped toward James's spot on the floor, where Beth was already kneeling.

"Hello," she was saying, a soft coo.

James's eyes fluttered, nearly opening.

"It's me, James. Open your eyes. It's me."

Slowly, like the unfurling of a cocoon, his eyes opened. It was not so peaceful, though, when he was on the edge of death.

"How do you feel?" I asked.

I had no idea what to do with him. What if he was in dire pain? Could I tear his stitches to try to pry the bullet out? Wouldn't that just make things worse?

All my months with the army, and I was useless here.

James smiled, his dark forehead wet with sweat.

"Thank you, Caleb," he said.

"What are you thanking me for? I haven't done much for you yet."

He shook his head.

"Thank you. And Tim?" Beth's eyes were watering. "Thank you, too."

Beth took his hand.

"Tell us how you feel, James. Tell us how you feel. Does it hurt? Does something hurt?"

"Don't worry." His breath was light, and his words were faint. "I'm all right."

Beth looked hopeful, but I knew what he really meant. He was at peace now. He knew what was coming.

It was a long few minutes, but Beth sat by his side and squeezed his hand as he drifted off. Her eyes were deep and haunted as if she had known pain like this before.

He grew still. There was an undeniable tranquility in it, and I was glad he'd had that: he seemed like the sort who would prefer to die slowly and peacefully rather than in the heat of the war. In war, I thought, one only had a moment to realize his fate before he was gone, and there was something excruciatingly slow about bleeding out, but James had been in such peace that I wondered how bad it could really be.

Time froze, so we stayed with him for a while. It was just the two of us staring down at his body. Maybe the few other negroes would come to pay their respects, and a few white men, too, but we were the only ones who would truly mourn him; we were the only ones who had known him. I regretted now that I had been so heartless with James's and Beth's friendship; it was unwise, yes, to consort with negroes, but that didn't matter now. He had been a man once—a good man—and I had never taken the opportunity to know him well.

After a good time had passed, we dragged the body out of the hospital to make room. The bodies of this afternoon were still scattered about the battlefield, so we brought him there. It wasn't too long a walk, really. This way, he would be buried with the other men. Beth was in agreement with this.

"He never would have wanted to die a soldier," she said, "but he would gladly have died fighting for his freedom."

Then, as we laid the body down among the others, she burst into tears.

It was our luck that we were alone for her weeping. She buried her head in my shoulder, and I held her until the first tears had dried on my coat, and still she shed more. I could not mourn him as strongly as she did, not when I hardly knew him, but her grief stirred my heart.

"He was a good friend to me," she muttered into my chest, still heaving with tears. "Whatever you thought of him, he was a good friend to me."

What could I say to that? *Well, I don't think it was a very good idea to be friends with him, and I'd say that again, but now that he's dead, I'm very sorry for you.* So I simply said, "I'm sorry." It wasn't enough, but it was the best I could do.

It was a long time. It was a long, long time. Eventually, she pulled her body free from mine, wiped away tears that showed no sign of ceasing, and said with trembling lips, "I want to leave, Cassie. I don't want to be a part of this anymore."

Was she intending to desert? No, she wouldn't. It was a simple complaint. Interestingly enough, this made sense to me. I could think of a thousand reasons why a girl like her would want to leave, but I couldn't think of a single reason why she had come in the first place, or why she decided to stay. Not any that made sense, anyway. So, in a way, this was a relief. I'd waited so long for the ice to finally break, for her to decide that this was too much for her and run away. If ever she was going to do that, it would be now, but she didn't. This was the best reason for her to go, but she stayed.

So she came back to the camp with tears in her eyes, and I was sorry for her—I truly was—but I felt a guilty inkling of relief, too. And that was how I knew I would never be good enough for her companionship.

Chapter Seventeen

It was odd how life just went on. The soldiers still ate and made merry as they did any other day. There was no funeral for James—the captain would never allow it when so many men died every day, and only a few people besides Beth and me seemed to be mourning him at all. Besides that moment, when he was laid to rest on the battlefield, I never saw her shed a single tear.

We had almost reached Savannah, and the excitement was nearly palpable. This was it; the end was near. Victory was certain. Even Beth was celebrating, and she had hardly smiled in the weeks since James's death.

"Where will you go when this is all over?" George was asking one of his crew, puffing out tobacco, same as ever.

"I think I'll try my luck in New York City." The fellow chuckled. "I'll never have to see this goddamned place again."

George shot him a dirty look for the cussword. The men here were a little rowdier than they were at home, but few of them were lax with their morals, and the rest of us were ever quick to shove them back in line.

"Ah, you won't find anything in New York. The wages are too low, and the Irish are too many. West is where I'm going. I'll get myself a woman, and a nice spot of land, and I'll be set for life. Doesn't that sound nice, boys?"

They all nodded eagerly.

"I say we set our sights for California!"

"There isn't a blasted speck of gold there anymore, if that's what you're thinking."

"Well, where else is there? Utah?"

"No, you fool. It's Oregon that you're looking for. Land as far as the eye can see and barely settled yet…"

And so it went on. As for me, the question hung in the air: Where would I go? I hardly had any money, but surely, a little cottage wouldn't be too much trouble. I *had* saved up a little bit—I hardly spent any of my paycheck for want of anything to waste it on. I wasn't rich, but I did have a sum.

In the town of Irwinton, we were sent out to prospect—so the captain called it—in case the villagers buried any of their valuables as so many before them had done. We each found medium-length sticks and began to poke at the fertile earth, hoping that buried treasure would sprout up as numerous as the cotton fields.

As it turned out, there was little. There were no slaves around to fill us in with secrets, and the people who were still there stubbornly refused to tell us anything.

I was poking about alone in someone's backyard when the woman herself came out in a fit of melodrama.

"My God! I cannot believe you all are here. What will happen to me? If you steal my belongings and pillage my home, what will I do?"

She was shielding her eyes from the sun as she addressed me, and she seemed honestly concerned with this question.

"What if I have to work? I suppose I could teach music lessons, but by God, I thought I would never be faced with such misfortune."

I glanced back at the house. I hadn't been oblivious, when I wandered onto this property, to the fact that the house was enormous, but I thought little of it. There were quite a few of them down here in the South. But even as wealthy as she seemed to be, had this woman truly never worked a day in her life? God, I had spent the last three years fighting for my brother's life and then mine, often laboring from dawn till dusk without a moment to wipe the sweat from my brow, and this lady actually thought I would be sympathetic to her complaints about teaching *music lessons*?

"I'm so dearly sorry, madam," I told her insincerely.

I had a feeling she wouldn't understand my tone.

She had wandered off her back porch; now she was close

enough that I could see the creases outside her eyes. She couldn't be older than forty, though.

"What if we lose this house?"

"In that case, I'm sure the music lessons will help sustain you, madam."

"Oh, God, don't even speak to me about it. I'm sorry that I brought it up. I simply can't stand the thought of it…the girls these days have no respect, no clue how to treat their elders. It would be a nightmare."

"I have felt blood soak into my hands as men died before my eyes," I thought. *"Do you honestly think you are seeing the worst of this war?"*

"Oh, believe me, madam, I know about nightmares. I can tell you about some of mine if you wish."

Her face twisted in distaste.

"I would rather not hear such things. I am a lady, you know."

So was I, once. But, I was never really a lady. I had used my two hands to work since the day I was born.

Using the stick, I came across an upturned bit of dirt.

"Is this where you hid your valuables, miss?"

She crossed her arms.

"I would never tell you."

"Well, I'll just find out for myself, then."

The woman was angry, I could tell, but she seemed more the sort to scream and storm off than try to wrestle me away—that might soil her dress. So I faced no real opposition in using my stick to prod some of the dirt away. If *this* lady was the one who had buried it, I wouldn't even need a shovel. She had probably buried it no more than a few inches deep.

And right I was. Less than an hour later, I emerged with the spoils of my effort: a box full of pearls and diamonds. The madam was still there, humming furiously as I took her treasure. I sifted a few pearl necklaces through my hands: I had never held something so expensive in my life. These Southern folk lived like nobles.

"*No!* Those are mine! The army is certainly not letting you steal from God-fearing American citizens!"

"You all seem to wish very dearly that you were not American," I replied acerbically. "And I did not steal from you. I never stepped foot into your house, and I never touched a hair on your pretty little head. I simply happened to stumble across this."

I gestured to one of the pearl necklaces.

"I wish you had buried some apples instead, maybe some bread, but the army will certainly find a way to use this."

Her face was turning red.

"God curse you, Yankee fools!"

"Good day, madam."

"You will regret this!" she cried. "God will curse you for what you have done to me!"

However, as I walked off the sprawling property with her precious jewelry in hand, she didn't even attempt to stop me.

We captured Savannah like this: less than three hundred yards away from the Rebels, we planted our cannons in the dirt and cocked our rifles, stared into the barrels of the Rebel guns, and waited for them to take the first shot. It was exhausting to hold up our Springfields all afternoon, but until we were given orders to put them down, there was nothing we could do but stand still as pine trees and wait.

The night was quiet and tense. Any second, they could start firing, and who knew how many they would take down before we had time to recover. When we gathered ourselves for the night, though, prepared to raise our rifles again in the morning, we were quite certain that we wouldn't even have to. It had been several hours, and unless they had some mighty reinforcements coming, they would have taken shots already if they were going to.

Thus it was: next morning, the buzz of the city beyond and the appealing glistening of the Atlantic were a steady background to what was really happening. The Rebels were retreating, horse-and-cart teams were being packed with supplies, men milled about dismantling tents and frowning at us. When they began their march away from us, away from the city of Savannah, they were met with the whoops and cheers of our victory. Like the rest of the Rebel South, the bustling city before our eyes was ripe for the taking.

Epilogue

Everywhere we went, we heard rejoicing. Every pub echoed low hums of laughter and merriment, and on the streets, the sound mingled with the chiming-bell laughs of the women. The American flag flew high over every establishment, especially the church. It soared over the countryside like a great ship's mast. Young boys shouted the news on every street corner while peddling and waving newspapers. Every city had sprung to life again; everyone in the nation was born anew.

"Charleston has never been like this," Beth murmured. "It was always a quiet city, at least compared to Richmond."

"No place is quiet now." I sighed.

"It's this way," she gestured.

On the outskirts of the city, the varied stones were laid in neat rows. I rearranged the small bouquet in my hands. There were four of them, actually. One for each grave.

Once we reached the cemetery, we both knelt before the unmarked ones in the back corner. These were soldiers' graves. There weren't many because very few died here in Charleston, but most likely, their families had brought them back here from wherever they fell.

None of these belonged to Beth's parents, or to Nick, or to Joshua, but we would honor the dead as if they were our own. Maybe somewhere, someone was doing the same for ours.

Beth concluded a heartfelt prayer: "And may God look upon you in Heaven as He did on Earth. Amen."

The graveyard was filled with a stillness like the calm after a storm.

"Is it really over?" I asked Beth, a question that had been buzzing in my head for days.

"I think so." She smiled sadly. "I think it really is."

About the Author

Chloe Helton lives in San Francisco, California. She has been writing historical fiction since the age of eleven, and she loves nothing more than wild, fictional heroines and a nice cup of tea.

Made in the USA
San Bernardino, CA
21 May 2017